William George Shaw

Memorials of the Clan Shaw

William George Shaw

Memorials of the Clan Shaw

ISBN/EAN: 9783337390044

Printed in Europe, USA, Canada, Australia, Japan

Cover: Foto ©Andreas Hilbeck / pixelio.de

More available books at **www.hansebooks.com**

𝕸𝖊𝖒𝖔𝖗𝖎𝖆𝖑𝖘

OF

THE CLAN SHAW.

BY

WILLIAM G. SHAW,

𝔍𝔫𝔠𝔲𝔪𝔟𝔢𝔫𝔱 𝔬𝔣 𝔖. 𝔍𝔬𝔥𝔫 𝔱𝔥𝔢 𝔈𝔟𝔞𝔫𝔤𝔢𝔩𝔦𝔰𝔱'𝔰 𝔆𝔥𝔲𝔯𝔠𝔥, 𝔉𝔬𝔯𝔣𝔞𝔯.

FIDE ET FORTITUDINE.

It is the voice of years that are gone,
The sound of days that are no more.—*Ossian.*

Na bean ris a chat gun lamhain.

PRINTED FOR PRIVATE CIRCULATION.

M.DCCC.LXXI.

CONTENTS.

" Nothing, as it appears to me, can be less rational than the vulgar scoff at Pedigree and Genealogy. The adage so constantly quoted by the antiquary, that no one who could lay claim to family antiquity ever despised it, undoubtedly meets with exceptions; but a reverence for the past, and a desire to establish a connection between it and self, are instinctive in human nature. And if instinctive, then rightly directed, they must be ennobling principles.

" Every family should have a record of its own. Each has its peculiar spirit, running through the whole line, and in more or less development perceptible in every generation. Rightly viewed, as a most powerful but much neglected instrument of education, I can imagine no study more rife with pleasure and instruction. Nor need our ancestors have been Scipios or Fabii to interest us in their fortunes. We do not love our kindred for their glory or for their genius, but for those domestic affections and private virtues, that, unobserved by the world, expand in confidence towards ourselves, and often root themselves, like the banian of the East, and flourish with independent vigour in the heart to which a kind Providence has guided them.

" An affectionate regard for the memory of our forefathers is natural to the heart; it is an emotion totally distinct from pride,—an ideal love, free from that consciousness of requited affection and reciprocal esteem, which constitutes so much of the satisfaction we derive from the love of the living.

" With what additional energy should the precepts of our parents influence us, when we trace the transmission of those precepts from father to son through successive generations, each bearing the testimony of a virtuous, useful, and honourable life, to their truth and influence; and all uniting in a kind and earnest exhortation to their descendants, so to live on earth, that (followers of HIM, through whose grace alone, we have power to obey HIM), we may at last be reunited with those who have been before, and those who shall come after us,—

> " No wanderer lost—
> A family in Heaven."

> —*Lord Lindsay's Lives of Lindsays*, vol. i. p. **xi**.

INTRODUCTION.

SINCE I printed the former portions of MEMORIALS OF THE SHAWS, I have obtained a large addition to my sources of information as to their bygone history.

I have thought it best to communicate the additional information which I have acquired, to my fellow clansmen and others who take an interest in the subject, in the form of a New Edition, which will nevertheless partake somewhat of the nature of a Second Part. To those who have not the former portions, this edition will supply as complete a History of the Clan as it is possible to compile, from the materials which have come into my possession. To those who have the former portions, it will be interesting to discover, to how a great an extent the accounts of our race, which came down to us by tradition, are confirmed by written records, and how many of the statements which I ventured to make on the ground of supposition, are proved by the evidence of the documents which have come into my possession, to be perfectly consistent with facts.

I assumed, for instance, from the fact that the Shaws, Macphersons, and Mackintoshes, were so closely united in the bonds of clanship, that they must also have been closely allied by the ties of intermarriages, (p. vi.). The truth of that assumption will be abundantly proved in the following pages.

Of course, when the Memorials are regarded as a whole, it is a disadvantage that the information they contain, should be given in such a detached and fragmentary manner, and that information given in the former portions should have to be repeated; but then again, it will be interesting to the members of the race, to see the process by which their past history was gradually recovered from the oblivion which had well nigh settled down upon it. I have had applications for the First Part of the Memorials, from Shaws of

A

whom I had never heard before, all over the world—India, Australia, Canada, and California. I have also had applications from those not of our own race or name, but who take an interest in matters connected with Clan history. As the First Part is out of print, I have not been able to respond to these applications. But in this Edition, enquirers will, I hope, find an exhaustive History of the Clan.

The sources from which I have drawn the information now given, and thus been able not only to confirm the general accuracy of what I have previously written, but to add very considerably to our knowledge of our forefathers, are three Manuscripts kindly lent to me by John Stuart, Esq., Secretary to the Society of Antiquaries. The originals of the MSS. belonging to Mr Stuart are in the possession of Cluny Macpherson. They are—

1.—"MEMOIRS, GENEALOGICAL and HISTORICAL of the FAMILY of MacINTOSH, with an Introduction concerning the Families of McDUFF, and Clan CHATTAN." The motto is "*Antiquam exquirite matrem.—*VIRGIL." Its date is 1758, and it embodies an older MS. dated in 1665.*

2.—"VANITIE EXPOSED, or a PLAIN and SHORT ANSWER to a late PAPER, intituled the GENEALOGIE of the FARQUHARSONS, wherein the Author's ignorance and self-contradictions are set in their true light, and the right Genealogy of that modern family briefly hinted at, from the concurring testimonies of the Shaws, the Farquharsons themselves, and all their neighbour families. In a LETTER to a FRIEND; by no enemy of theirs but a friend to truth, Sir Æneas Macpherson of Invereshie, Knight." The motto is,

* I think there is good reason for coming to the conclusion, that the author of the 1758 MS. was the Rev. Lachlan Shaw, the Historian of Moray. In the Spalding Club vol. "Family of Rose of Kilravock" there is quoted a document by the Historian on the "Chieftainre" of Clan Chattan, which is evidently an abridged version of what is said in the MS. on the same subject. Then again, the only genealogy of Shaws given in the MS. besides that of the principal family, is that of the Shaws of Dell, to which family the Rev. Lachlan Shaw belonged; and, lastly, it quotes largely from the Cawdor and other Charter Chests. And, as Mr Stuart remarked to me, no one could have done this at the time, except the Historian.

" Answer a fool in his folly, least he be wise in his own conceit.—
SOLOMON."

3.—The third is a Manuscript, bearing the title " MACPHERSONS,"
and contains Notes concerning the Claims of the Head of that
Race to the Chieftainrie of Clan Chattan, with copious Genealogies
of its different branches, circa 1680.   It seems to be an abridgment
of a larger MS. by Sir Æneas Macpherson, which I have not seen,
but from which I have seen quotations made in works relating to
the Highlands of Scotland.

The general accuracy of those Manuscripts is proved by the
fact, that their statements and the steps in the Genealogies which
they furnish, are confirmed in a remarkable manner by the evidence
of various kinds of documents, Bonds of Manrent, &c., recovered
from the Charter Chests in which they have been long buried, and
published in the invaluable volumes of the Spalding Club, more
particularly in the volumes entitled, *"the Thanes of Cawdor,"* and the
" Family of Rose of Kilravock."   The Thanes of Cawdor and the
Roses were much associated of old in all sorts of transactions,
sometimes friendly, sometimes hostile, with the Clan Chattan.

Chapter First.

FROM what I have previously written, as well as from what follows, it must be evident to all that there are two different accounts of the origin of the Shaws, some deriving them only from Shaw Mor Coriaclich,* the Captain of the thirty of the Clan Quhele who fought on the North Inch at Perth ; others insisting that they existed as a powerful clan in the district of Rothiemurchus, for a century previous. Those who hold the latter view plead the tradition common to the Shaws and the Comyns, of bloody contests previous to that time—a tradition which has found its most recent embodiment in the magnificent volume published some months ago, entitled Memorials of the Bruces and the Cummings. They insist also, that the Statement of the Mackintoshes, that Shaw Mor was not the chief of an allied Clan, but a Cadet of their own family is not true, and that the place assigned to him in their Genealogy as *Shaw MacGilchrist MacIan*, (Shaw the son of Gilchrist the son of Ian, said Ian being brother of William, (VIIth) Chief of Mackintoshes, is a clumsily devised invention, whereby the name of the leader of the clan Yha (the Christi Johnson or Christi MacIan of Wyntoun,)† with the name Shaw prefixed to it, is made to do duty for Sha Ferquharson, the name of the leader of the clan Quhele. If, (they ask) Shaw MacGilchrist MacIan, was the name of the captain of the victorious party, what was the name of the leader of the van-

---

* Coriaclich is pronounced with the accent on the second syllable.

† The words of Wyntoun, the only contemporaneous historian, are—

> They three score were clannys twa,
> Clahynne Quhele and Clachin Yha,
> And there they had thair chiftanys twa ;
> Scha Farquharis Sone was ane of thay,
> The tother Christy Johnesone.

quished? It is of course necessary to their supposition to maintain that the " *Shaw Farquhar's Son* " of Wyntoun is the same with the " *Shaw MacGilchrist MacIan,*" of their Genealogy, only that Wyntoun gives him the name of his more remote ancestor, whilst their Genealogy designates him by the the name of his father and grandfather. And thus we have all the names given by Wyntoun, exhausted in the designation of the Mackintosh Candidate for the honours of the day. What, it is enquired, was the name of his opponent? They point also to the mention of *Sheah et omnes Clan Quhele** in the Scots Act of Parliament of 1392, four years before the date of the battle. They allege that the notice in a deed† of 1338, of a *manerium quondam Scayth* (or Shaw) *filii Ferchardi,* in the district of Rothiemurchus, and of a Seth or Shaw father of a Ferchard, as a witness in a deed of 1234, points to the occupation of Rothiemurchus by Shaws and not by Mackintoshes. It is only subsequent tradition, they say, which gives him the appellation " Shaw Macintosh." In two deeds of the period, he appears as *Scayth* or *Seth*, both pronounced according to Gaelic analogies, *Shaw.*

If the Clan Quhele and the Clan Chattan, were one and the same, how comes it that the Clans are entered separately in a Scots Act of Parliament in 1594? So late as that period, we have a Clan Quhele, entered in an Act of Parliament, as distinct from the Clan Chattan, and it may be added, distinct also from the Macphersons. The Clan Chattan and the Clan Quhele are both mentioned together, which looks however as if they were closely allied races. Now we have abundant evidence to prove the existence of a race of Shaws, from time immemorial, in close association with the Mackintoshes, but in no Act are they mentioned as Shaws; only once does the name Sha crop out as the leader of the Clan Quhele, in the Scots Act of Parliament of 1392.

The Shaws, however, were quite as worthy of the denunciations of the Act of 1594, as the Mackintoshes and Macphersons; for in

---

* Quhele is sometimes spelt *Chewill.*

† Charter by the Earl of Ross, of Dalnafert and Kinrorayth (Kinrara) reserving an acre of ground near the Stychan of Dalnafort *in qua situm fuit mancrium quondam* SCAYTH *filii Ferchardi.—Pref. to Spald. Club Misc.,* p. xxvi.

1680, a century later, they are spoken of as "a tribe of able fighting "men, headed by Alexander Shaw, and fighting under the banner of "Mackintosh."* The conclusion therefore (it is pleaded) is, that they were the race meant to be hunted down, as "broken men," under the designation of Clan Quhele, and that the Shaws were that branch of the Clan Chattan known in days of old by that name, a Clan so closely allied to the Mackintoshes, as almost to be regarded as a junior branch of their Clan, under a different designation, which accounts for the Mackintoshes claiming the honours of the contest. True, the Shaws have utterly lost all record of their ever having been called the Clan Quhele, as indeed many of them (in part fulfilment it may be, of the blight decreed against them for their ancestor Allan's sin,) had almost lost all memory of their ever having been a Highland Clan. But no other Clan can produce any evidence that it was ever called the Clan Quhele. True, it has been alleged, that the Camerons were the Clan Quhele of the contest; not because it can be shown that they were ever called by that name, but because there is a tradition that they were one of the parties engaged in it. But then again the invincible evidence of authentic records, it is argued, is against this claim, for the Camerons are entered in the Act above alluded to, as a Clan *distinct* from the Clan Quhele. It is, therefore, concluded that the Clan Quhele was the designation of that branch of the Clan Chattan, known latterly as a junior branch of the Mackintoshes under the name of Shaws.

And, as I wrote in *Notes and Queries*, in October 1869 :—

"This conclusion is still further fortified by the following considerations:—After 1594 we find no mention made in any contemporary record of the Clan Quhele: it drops out of history. About this very period the Shaws were "broken up" as a Clan, on account of the slaughter of his step-father, Dallas of Cantray, by Allan their chief, and the subsequent forfeiture of the latter. Henceforward they followed the banner of Mackintosh, and several of the principal cadets of the family migrated to Deeside and Forfarshire. And (what is very important) it is *not until the beginning of the 16th century* that historians introduce the name of the Clan Chattan as one of the contending parties on the Inch ; and why,

* Sir Robert Sibbald's MS., in Advocates Library.

but because the Clan Quhele was but a branch of this powerful confederacy; and the Mackintoshes, as principals of the Clan Chattan, got the credit in the 16th century of what had been done in former days by the Clan Quhele."

Against all this, it is argued by the Mackintoshes, that for two centuries at least, they have been regarded as parties to the conflict, under the designation of Clan Chattan; and that when the later historians spoke of the Clan Chattan having fought against the Clan Cay or the Clan Yha, they *meant*, and could mean no other than the Mackintoshes—that the Mackintoshes have a history more or less authentic, and certainly much more minute and detailed than that of the Shaws, and that, as Mr Mackintosh Shaw says in *Notes and Queries*—" Their traditions and records are more entitled to credit than the statements of Wyntown and other contemporary chroniclers, in as much as Wyntown only recorded the matter on report, and really knew so little of the matter, that he distinctly says he did not know which side won."

" Quha had the ware thare at the last
I will nocht say."

The allegations of the Mackintoshes are supported by the testimony of Sir George Macpherson in his " VANITIE EXPOSED :"—He says :—

"I am very positive that there never was a Shaw in Rothiemurchus till Robert the 3rd's time. That Shaw Corriacklach, Macintosh's 3rd or 4th son, took possession on't by consent of the Clan Chattan of Baden·ach (meaning by the Clan Chattan the Macphersons) who, long ere this, had nearly extirpated the Cummines, by several eminent victories obtained against them, and in fine killed a small fragment that remained at *Lagnan Cuimenach* in Strathspey; and, if I err in this, I err with the constant traditions of the Shaws themselves, and their neighbour families. For this it was, that the bloody hand and dagger was added to their (the Macphersons' bearing), as Sir George Mackenzie expressly has it, in his Book of Heraldry, which the Laird of Mackintosh after that assumed to himself as their pretended Chief, and the Shaws thereafter as come of him, when they began to pretende to armes."

He goes on, in answer to the claim of the Farquharsons to be descended from a son of Shaw Coriaclich's, thus :—

" 'That this Shaw Corriaclich was a son of the Laird of Mackintosh's, and that he possessed Rothiemurchus after the Ruine of the Cummines, has been received and uncontroverted tradition, of all the families of the North since the Shaws were known. But how he makes, or can make, him the eleventh from MacDuff, except as come of Macintoshe, he leaves to the Reader's conjecture, for he himself knew nothing of the matter. But that their (the Farquharson's Farquhar) who went first not to Mar but to Braymar a full age after this, was neither son nor grandson to Shaw Corriaclich, but a remote Cadet of Shaw of Dell, who was a Cadet of Shaw of Rothiemurchus is positively affirmed by the Shaws themselves."

The writer, whose statements Sir Æneas controverts, having claimed the "Chieftainrie" of both Farquharsons and Shaws for the then FARQUHARSON of INVERCAULD, Sir Æneas answers him thus :—

" 1. Either Mackintosh as lineally and lawfully representing the great MacDuff must be Chief of all his descendants; or if, because of their different names, he is restricted to be Chief of the Mackintoshes only, it follows *a pari* by a necessary consequence, that Farquharson must lose the Shaws, Farquhars, MacEundlas, &c., and restrict his Chiefship to the Farquharsons only.

" 2. This Farquhar (the Farquharson's ancestor) was not at all a son of Shaw Coriaclich's; but according to the constant and received tradition of the Shaws, a son . . . of a Cadet of Shaw of Dell. . . . ROTHIEMURCHUS' issue male cannot be extinct, whilst there is a Shaw in a direct line extant of the family of Daill; so that if there be any Chieftainrie in the case, distinct from Mackintosh's, as I think there cannot, it belongs to Shaw of Daill."*

The writer, in the interest of the Farquharsons, having stated, that the Shaws and Farquharsons carried the fir-tree in their arms "from ane ancient custom of bearing twigs of fir for their sign and badge in time of battle ;" Sir Æneas is again down upon him, thus : " That the fir-tree," he writes, "in this coat is taken as a principall bearing, for the reason given by this Scribbler, is a bare pretence. For the Shaws and after them the Farquharsons themsel-

* Sir Æneas had been ignorant of the existence of the branch of the ancient family of Rothiemurchus resident in Deeside, headed by the ancestor of the branch of Shaws of which the Compiler is a member, Lord Mar's Chamberlain, DUNCAN OF CRATHINARD.

res always wore a tuft of heath or heather, and added the fir-tree to the Clan Chattan's and Mackintosh' his arms, only as a mark of Cadency, and in commemoration of Rothiemurchus from whence they came, and where grow so many firs."

Thus writes Sir Æneas, of whose spirited and lengthy Essay on this subject, I have given a véry imperfect idea from the extracts above quoted.

I may mention, that his statement as to the origin of the Farquharsons is confirmed by the Brouchdearg MS. quoted in Part I. of these Memorials. This Manuscript traces them back no farther than the grandfather of *Findla Mór*, who fought at the Battle of Pinkie, thus leaving a gap of several generations between the time of their first progenitor and *Shaw Mór Coriaclich*.

The writer of the Mackintosh MS. as might be expected from the nature of his subject, undertaking as he does to give accounts, so far as he is able, of all the various branches of the Clan Chattan, is much more voluminous. His own MS. was written probably about 1758. The Mackintosh MS. on which he founds, and which he embodies in his own, correcting it by the evidence of charters and other documents as he proceeds, brings down the history of the Mackintoshes to 1665.

With reference to the matter last above noticed, he quotes Mr Nisbet in his "Marks of Cadency," as saying, that Invercauld bears the LION OF MACDUFF, being descended of Shaw of Rothiemurchus before the year 1500 ; for Finlay More, the 3rd in descent, was killed at the Battle of Pinkie, A.D. 1547.

His account of the origin of the Shaws is as follows :—

" Rothiemurchus was very early Church land, for King Alexander II. gave it to Andrew, Bishop of Moray, in exchange for other lands, Anno Regni XII. A.D. 1226, (Chart. Mor.), and the Shaws had possession of it so early, that they joined in King David Bruce's reign in cutting off the Cumyns, (and on that account INVERCAULD bears a dexter hand grasping a dagger, as Mr Nisbet quotes from the Lyon's Register) ; but having only a lease from the Bishop, when the lease expired, Cumming of Altyre took a lease of it, and obtained possession of it by cutting off Shaw of Rothiemurchus and his family ; and he built the Castle of Rothiemurchus in Loch-an-Eilan, and for several years made it his sum-

B

mer dwelling. Shaw (afterwards called Shaw Coriaclich) was a child in the house of his grandfather by the mother's side (viz., a daughter of Baron Fergusson in Athole), when his father and friends were killed by Altyre; and when he came of age, gathering a company of Shaws and Fergussons, he led them into Rothiemurchus, resolving to revenge the death of his father and friends. They lurked in a thicket wood near to Auchnahaitnich for some nights, until they understood that Altyre was on his way coming up, and that thicket is to this day called *Preas na Mearlach*, "the Robber's Thicket," at the foot of a little hill called Callort; and being informed by a watch placed on that hill, that Altyre took the road, on the north side of the Loch of Pitteulish, they removed to a hollow full of wood by the roadside (still called Lag-na-Cuimenach) and surprised Altyre and his company and cut them all off, upon which they repossessed themselves of Rothiemurchus.

"This tradition, supported by such standing Memorials," says the writer of the Manuscript, "is very strong."

On concluding the history of the Mackintoshes, the writer of the MS. resumes the subject of the incorporated Clans, who "were called Clan Chattan, for several generations," and of whom Mackintosh was designed Captain. "These are," says the writer, "The Macphersons, Clan Dabhi, MacBains, Macphails, MacGillivrays, MacQueens, Smiths, Clarkes, MacIntyres, and Shaws."

Under section "THE SHAWS," he thus writes :—

"Those of this name reside in the South West, in the North, and in the Western Isles of Scotland, besides several gentlemen of fortune in England and the North West of Ireland."

After alluding to what he had already said as to the opinion of learned antiquarians as to their orgin, he goes on :—

"At what precise time, or from what particular Thane of Fife they descended, I pretend not to determine, if we can rely on the testimony of Boece and Abercrombie, their descent from MacDuff must have been very early. I question not but the Shaws of the South were the stock of the name, for MacDuff, their ancestor having his seat of residence in the South, probably his son Shiach or Shaw would have settled near to his paternal family."

Here follows the Genealogy of the Shaws of Sauchie. In the opinion of the present writer, the Shaws of the South are a distinct and independent race. They never acknowledged Mackintosh as

their Chief, or claimed to be counted with the Clan Chattan Confederacy. There is no trace of any such connection in the Coats of
Arms borne by the respective races.

According to Sir Æneas Macpherson :—

" The Shaws of Sauchie flatly deny any interest in MacDuff, or that
ever they came from Rothiemurchus, or the North, and as to this last
part, with a deal of reason too, for they have charters of King William
the Lyon, who was 300 years at least or ever there was a Shaw in
Rothiemurchus."

The Mackintosh MS. of 1665, embodied in the other, enunciates
the Mackintosh theory as to the origin of the Shaws, coinciding
generally also with that of Sir Æneas Macpherson. Under the
head of Lachlan, (VIIth) Chief, it gives an account of the Clan Battle
at Perth, and of the circumstances which led to it. It states that
the opponents of the Clan Chattan (Mackintoshes) were the Clan
Cay, a branch of the Cummines. The Commentator and Compiler
(of 1758) insists, in opposition to this, that they were the Clan
Dabhi, *Dabhi* in Gaelic being equivalent to *Yai*, and Yai would of
course be the *Yha* of Wyntoun.

The original MS., 1665, at the conclusion of the account of the
Clan Battle, gives the usual Mackintosh version of the story, as to
Mackintosh having given to Shaw his cousin, * the lands of
Rothiemurchus, on account of the valour he exhibited that day.

Commenting on this, the transcriber of the MS., in 1758, main-
tains, that " as to Mackintosh giving them possession of his lands of
Rothiemurchus, immediately after the conflict at Perth, as it is
vouched only by the author of the MS., so it is inconsistent with
invaried tradition," which tradition, he goes on to give, as already
quoted at page 13.

Before giving the tradition, however, he allows that the fact that
he had found Alexander Kiar Shaw of Rothiemurchus, designated as " Alexander Mackintoshe of Rothiemurchus," in a deed
of 1482, may favour to some extent the Mackintosh theory, that the
Shaws were descended of the Mackintoshes. The deed is an in-
denture, whereby the Thane of Cawdor and Huchone Ross, Baron
of Kilravock, bind themselves in amity, and for the furtherance

* Sir Æneas makes him his son, p. 11.

thereof, that a son of the Thane's shall marry a daughter of the Baron's. Alexander Mackintosh of Rothiemurchus, and Thomas le Grant of the Cathedral Kirk of Moray, are appointed Arbiters (*Thanes of Cawdor*, p. 64.)

The writer of the MS. of 1758, speaks of but one deed in which Alexander Kiar (or " Swarthy ") of Rothiemurchus was so designated. He is so designed, however, in several deeds of the period : in a Bond of Man Rent to the Earl of Errol in 1472 ; in a Bond between " Duncan Mackintosh, Capitane of Clan Quhattane, his son Ferchard, and the Baron of Kilravock," in 1481, to which the seal of Alister Kiar is affixed, and in another deed of a similar nature, dated 17th June 1490.*

In writing the First Part of these Memorials, I fell into a mistake as to this Alexander Mackintosh, Thane of Rothiemurchus. I concluded that he was at that time Captain or Chief of Clan Chattan, not having adverted to the fact, proved alike by the Mackintosh Genealogies and by abundant documentary evidence, that during the time Alister Kiar was Thane of Rothiemurchus, the Chieftianrie of Clan Chattan was held by Duncan, who, with his son Ferquhard is, as we have seen, mentioned in several deeds of the period. But it appears, on subsequent research, that he was the grandson of Coriaclich and a Shaw. Amidst divergences of various kinds as to the steps and names in their Genealogies, this is found invariably recorded as a settled point. There may be a dispute as to who Coriaclich was, whether he was a relation of the Chief of the Mackintosh, or the leader of a distinct though " consanguineous " Clan,

---

* See " Family of Rose of Kilravock," and " Thanes of Cawdor," *passim*. Mr Cosmo Innes, tells us that the seal of Alister Kiar Mackintosh is to a great extent obliterated. In the 1st and 4th quarters, he traces the lion rampant. In the 2nd and 3d " probably," he says, " bezants 3, 2, & 1." This apparent arrangement of bezants had doubtless been the remains of what had once been pine trees, thus—

"three and two" being the branches, and " one" part of the trunk. The shield also bears, he says, three Mullets. As " Mullets " were always used as a mark of cadency, this would go to show that Alister Kiar, Thane of Rothiemurchus, was nevertheless only a Cadet of the House of Mackintosh.

but there is no dispute as to the steps and names in the Genealogy of the race of which he was the progenitor.

In all the Genealogies of the Shaws, as given by the Mackintoshes, we find—first, Shaw Coriaclich, then James Shaw, son to Coriaclich, then Alister Kiar, from whom the Shaws of Delnavert and Daill trace their descent. The Mackintosh MS. of 1665, in its account of the Battle of Harlaw, states that "the only two persons of distinction who fell on the side of Donald of the Isles, were MacLean of Dowart, and James Shaw of Rothiemurchus." The Mackintoshes admit that Alexander Kiar, though signing himself by the patronymic "Mackintosh," was a Shaw, and the grandson of Coriaclich, only they urge that the circumstance of his being called Mackintosh, proves the truth of their version of the story of the Clan Battle at Perth, and of the origin of the Shaws ; showing, they allege, the recent change of surname, if indeed it had been changed at all at that time, from Mackintosh to Shaw.

Against this theory might be set a version of the Clan Battle by Mr Hew Rose, the biographer in 1683, of the "Family of Rose of Kilravock."

"He that fought" (*i.e.* commanded) "the Clan Chattan, is said to have been the 3rd in succession, and being formerly surnamed Shaw Mackintosh, he took the patronymic only, as descended from the Thanes of Fife, for his surname, *not using that of Shaw any more.*" (Spald. Club vol., p. 41.)

If this statement of Mr Hew Rose be the true account of the story, then previous to 1396, Coriaclich, though descended from MacDuff no less than the Mackintoshes, (Sons of the Thane,) had contented himself, like his predecessors, with the name of Shaw. After the Clan Battle, he dropped the Shaw, and took the more aristocratic designation "Mackintosh," *i.e.* "SON OF THE THANE." His son Hamish (James), however, still retained the name Shaw, and as a Shaw his name comes down to us as one of the distinguished persons slain at the battle of Harlaw. The "swarthy" (Kiar) Alexander succeeds, and no doubt, adding land to land, and field to field, and his family and vassals increasing, becomes of sufficient importance to be designated as Thane of Rothiemurchus.

He would then naturally prefer the appellation Mackintosh to that of Shaw, as being the more aristocratic. * But when his son Ian succeeded, the old name had been resumed, probably for the sake of distinguishing the families at Rothiemurchus from the chief branch of the Mackintoshes.†

There is, however, another theory which may be the true solution of the difficulty :—That there was a race consanguineous to the Mackintoshes, descended equally with them from the great Thane, called sometimes by the patronymic Mackintosh, and sometimes also at first, Clan Quhele,‡ that this Clan fought in the Raid of Angus under Sheach, and again in the Clan Battle at Perth ;§ that subsequent to this time, the members of this Clan, though often designating themselves by the patronymic Mackintosh, began to be called Shaws ; that this name became fixed as their surname in the fourth generation from Coriaclich ; and that in the tradition of the Clans, deeds of valour which had previously been spoken of as done by the Clan Quhele, came to be spoken of as having been done by the Shaws ; that on the utter break up of the Clan Quhele about 1580, the Chroniclers began to attribute the share taken by

---

* We find an Ian McAllan McIan Keyr, subscribing a Bond to Sir John Campbell, in 1519. He may have been the grandson of Ian above mentioned, the genealogy, after Alister Kiar, running thus—Alister Kiar, father of Ian, father of Allan, father of Ian. (Thanes of Cawdor, p. 130.)

† Mr A. Mackintosh Shaw writes to me as to the above extract from the " Family of Rose of Kilravock," thus :— "I have always looked upon it, as one of the most confused bits of writing extant. The man who wrote it, knew little or nothing of the matter. He speaks of the Clan Chattan under *Mackintosh's predecessor*, which is wrong. He had some dim idea that the victorious leader was a grandson of, or 3rd in succession from somebody, and so he puts him down 3rd in succession, by which he no doubt means 3d Chief of Mackintosh. Then again he knew that the leader was named Shaw, and that he was a Mackintosh, and so he gives him a *double surname*, which is quite a modern invention ; and as he called him *Mackintosh's* predecessor, and knows that he dropped *one* name, he is obliged to make him drop that of Shaw to be consistent. I do not think that what the writer says, is worth anything whatever, or that anything can be got from it, except an illustration of the ease with which tradition gets twisted and altered, especially when it gets into the hands of those who have no interest in it."

‡ Scots Act of Parliament.

§ Wyntoun.

the Clan Quhele in the Clan Battle at Perth, to the consanguineous and then powerful race, (of which the Clan Quhele was but a branch) the Clan Chattan.

The idea of two allied and related but distinct Clans, both in reality "Mackintoshes," "as sons of the Thane," the one called Clan Chattan, the other Clan Quhele, is fortified by the fact, that we find the race inhabiting Rothiemurchus in the 15th century, headed by one so powerful as to be called a Thane, Alister Kiar. Is it likely that one in the position of Thane would not have a Clan and "following" of his own, "*his hunder pipers an a' an a',*" as well as the "Capitane of the Clan Quhattane?"

That there is a mist hanging over the story of the Clan Battle on the Inch at Perth, bound up as it is with the origin of the Shaws, in spite of all that has been adduced, must be evident to all. We find writers on different sides of the question, quoting "unvaried tradition," as being in their favour, some (as for instance the author of the Mackintosh MS. of 1758, and the Historian of Moray,) alleging an unvaried tradition for the existence of the Shaws, previous to the Clan Battle, others, an "unvaried tradition," as for instance, Sir Æneas Macpherson, and the earlier Mackintosh MSS., that they spring only from Coriaclich. But the tradition that they have had an existence and a local habitation—at least since *the days of Coriaclich*—no one denies. That tradition is really "*unvaried.*"

The Macphersons claim to have been the branch of the Clan Chattan who were victorious on the field, and they produce the black Chanter of the Bagpipes, which the angel of victory (probably S. Catan,) dropped down amongst them on the occasion, and which they still retain (*quantum valeat*) as an evidence of the fact! But they, as well as the Mackintoshes, admit, that they were led by Shaw Mor Coriaclich. The Mackintoshes account for their having been so led, by the statement that Lauchlan their chief was an old man, and that Shaw Coriaclich had for some years previously led the Clan, as for instance at the Raid of Angus, where, according to the Scots Act he took part with *omnes Clan Quhele*. The Macphersons account for their having been led by Shaw, from the fact, which both sides seem to admit, that Shaw was married to

Jane, daughter of the then chief of the Macphersons,* Donald More, "Clunie's ancestor," as he is called by the author of the Mackintosh MS. of 1758. It is the same writer who tells us, that the name of the daughter of the Macpherson Chief, who was married to Coriaclich, was Jane.

The very disputes as to our existence previous to the date of the Clan Battle at Perth, prove our existence as a distinct sept after that period, and our connection through Coriaclich with that contest. The Macphersons and Mackintoshes deny that we fought as a Clan, but both allow that they were led by a Shaw, who was the founder of our race. Some may ask, why take all this trouble to prove such a matter?

It is answered, that it is a matter as to which there has been a great deal of literary contention amongst far more illustrious branches of the Clan Chattan, than the Shaws; and they may therefore be allowed to have a share in that literary contest now, with so much to urge in support of their having had a hand in the real fray, which gave occasion to it.

And I will add, that it cannot be a matter of indifference to any race or Clan, to be able to assert its claims to a share in an incident, which has been immortalized by the pen of Sir Walter Scott.

---

* The Douglas Baronage and the Macpherson MS., differing though they do in many particulars, agree in making Donald More chief at this time.

Chapter Second.

THE ANCIENT FAMILY OF ROTHIEMURCHUS AND ITS BRANCHES.

I SHALL now proceed to put on record the traces of our race, which I have discovered in the MSS. above-mentioned, subsequent to the time of Alexander Kiar Shaw. The Mackintosh MS. of 1758, tells us that " The unvaried tradition of the countrie beareth, that Alister Kiar had five sons, viz., John (or Ian), his successor ; James More, ancestor to Shaw of Dell ; Ferquhard, of whom the Farquharsons are come ; Robert, ancestor to Shaw of Tordarroch ;* and William, ancestor of Delnafert."

John of Rothiemurchus married Eupheme Mackintosh, daughter of Allan, brother of Duncan, (XIth) Laird of Mackintosh.

In another part of the Manuscript, it is stated that this Allan was married to Catherine, daughter of Hugh, Lord Lovat, that he lived at Bellachranich, in Stratherrick, and that he had five sons, viz., Lachlan, William, John, Alexander, and Hutcheon. Hutcheon it is stated, married Marion, daughter of the Thane of Cawdor. The general accuracy of the MS. is incidentally confirmed, by the fact, that the " Bande of Marriage " between the said " Huchone Allanson," and the said Marion is still extant, and is printed in " *The Thanes of Cawdor*," p. 73. It is dated 20th August, 1490.

---

* The Shaws of Tordarroch themselves, trace their descent from an uncle of Alister Kiar's— Adam, brother of James Shaw. But the remote steps of ancient genealogies must always be liable to such variations, having come down for centuries by oral tradition. One ancestor is often apt to be put in place of another, especially by the members of collateral branches, who of course do not know the descent of other branches so well as that of their own. My friend, Dr George J. Shaw, used to confound his great-grandfather, Duncan of Cortachy, with Duncan of Cortachy's grandfather, Duncan of Crathinard.

C

The parties to it are—" Vylyame Thayne of Caldor, on the one part, and Doncanc Mackintoshe Capitane of the Clancattane, Fearchar M'Intosche sone and aperand ayr [heir] to the foresaid Doncane and Huchone Allansone." The witnesses are—" Master Thomas the Grant Official of Murra, Vilyame Doles [Dallas] Canttra [Cantray], Alexander Allanson, brother to the said Huchone, Bean Makimpersone, wyth divers sindri." The lady's portion was "*fourty* pundis of the usuall mone of Scotlande."

It is interesting to find the MS. thus confirmed by authentic evidence. It states, also, that Allan had two daughters, besides the one married to Ian-Mac-Alister-Kiar Shaw of Rothiemurchus, viz., Renille, married to Alexander Mackintosh, and Mary to Robertson of Lude.

To return to the genealogies of the Shaws. The MS. proceeds to state that, John of Rothiemurchus was succeeded by his son Allan, who married a daughter of Ferchard, (XII<u>th</u>) Laird of Mackintosh. Turning to the Mackintosh Genealogy in the same MS., we find that this Ferchard (mentioned in the above quoted Contract of Marriage) married Giles Fraser, daughter of Lord Lovat, and by her had four daughters, viz., one married to Allan Shaw of Rothiemurchus ; another, Janet, married to the Laird of Guthrie; another to Strachan of Glenkindie; and another to Alister MacAllan, chief of Clan Ranald. The Laird of Guthrie above mentioned was David, son of Sir Alexander Guthrie. Both father and son fell at Flodden in 1513.*

Allan Shaw was succeeded by John (sixth in descent from Coriaclich). " This gentleman," says the MS., " married—— Campbell, and by her had Allan and other sons."

Allan was the last Shaw who held the lands of Rothiemurchus. The MS. proceeds to tell us how he lost his heritage.

How the Shaws lost Rothiemurchus.

" In this gentleman's time, in the end of the 16th century, the Shaws lost the lands of Rothiemurchus in the manner following. Allan, a batchelor, resided in Balnespick, a part of his estate. His mother (who

* See Guthrie Genealogy, in Burke's Landed Gentry, vol. ii. p. 416.

to her second husband married Dallas of Cantray,* in Strathnairn) lived in the Doune of Rothiemurchus. The young gentleman desired that his mother and step-father should resign in his favour, the Doune, which was then the seat of the family, but Cantray would not agree to it. This discord, aggravated by other circumstances, was barbarously resented by Allan ; for, chancing to meet Cantray on the public road, south of the Doune, he assaulted and murdered him, in a hollow called to this day *Lag-an-Dalasich.* For this heinous crime, aggravated by his connection with Dallas, Allan was prosecuted and outlawed."

It may here be noted, that there must have been some powerful influence at work, to procure Allan's outlawry and forfeiture on account of slaughtering Dallas. In those days, there were ways of evading the consequences of such crimes, when the perpetrators were rich or had a considerable " following," as evidenced in the Note at the foot of this page. The more powerful Grants had doubtless cast longing eyes on Rothiemurchus ; and Allan's crime had been turned to account, as the means to enable them to obtain possession of the " Jezreel " which they coveted.

If Allan had been more able to cope with that powerful Clan, he would never have lost Rothiemurchus for killing his stepfather. Hence, perhaps, the strong feeling entertained in the district for ages against his dispossession. Probably the murder of himself by the Grants, as afterwards noticed, had added to this feeling.

To return to the Manuscript :—

" Keeping with him a company of daring and desperate men, Allan could not be apprehended, and he still levied the rents of Rothiemurchus. John Grant of Freuchie purchased Allan's forfeiture and escheat, but could not get peaceable possession of the lands, upon which, Patrick Grant of Muckerach, uncle to Freuchie, excambed with his nephew the lands of Muckerach for those of Rothiemurchus ; and yet, tho' he was a

* The Dallases of Cantray were at one time a very powerful family. In " The Thanes of Cawdor " their names are constantly occurring alongside of Roses, Dunbars, Frasers, Mackintoshes, and Gordons, &c. Under date 31st May, 1513, " Henry Doles of Cantray, John of Doles, brither german to umquhil Archibald Doles, quhome God assoilze, along with Huchon Ross of Kilraok, " and others, sign a letter of " assythment " or acquittance for the slaughter of said Archibald by Robert Stewart of Clauok. " Suffragis [prayers] were done for the saule of the said Archibald." Cantray's seal is a fess between three stars, p. 184.

brave and bold man, he could obtain no peaceable possession during the life of Allan, who wasted the lands of Rothiemurchus, and the lands on Wester Dulanan above Duthel. At length, Mackintoshe of Strone, Allan's confidant, betrayed him into the hands of a party of Grants in the silence of the night, at *Lag-na-Calrich*, on the confines of Badenoch and Strathspey, from whence he was carried to Castle Grant, was civilly entertained, conveyed to his room at night, and found dead in his chair in the morning. Then Patrick of Muckerach had peaceable access to the lands, and Allan's brother and associates exiled into the Western Isles and Ireland, where their descendants are said to live in opulent circumstances. This traditional account I have from men of probity, whose fathers lived in the time of these transactions. Thus the direct line of the Shaws of Rothiemurchus became extinct in this country, and the nearest colateral branch was Shaw of Dell."

The writer of the MS. had not known of the branch of Shaws, located first at Crathinard in Deeside, and, at the time he wrote, in Glenisla; tracing their descent from Alister Ruadh, brother of Allan.

Shaws of Dell.

The following is the genealogy of the Shaws of Dell, (or as it is sometimes spelt "Daill") as given in the MS. (1) James More, father of (2) James Beg, father of (3) Alexander, father of (4) Alister Oge (or Oig), father of (5) John MacAlister Oge, father of (6) John Oge, father of (7) Alexander, father of Robert and of (8) James who died at Delnavert in 1758.

The general accuracy of the above Genealogy is confirmed by notices of Shaws of Dell in various authentic records. In the second volume of the Spalding Club Miscellany, (p. 128), we have "John MacAlister, in Dell of Rothemurkus," (5th in the above Genealogy) appearing in a way, perhaps not very much to his credit. On 19th July, 1594—"before the Court of Regality of Spynie,"— he was "decerned by the judge—ryplie aduysit with the action of spuilzie persewit contrane him be the Baron of Kincardine, . . . to have vrongouslie intromittit with and detenit the broune horse lybellit, and thairfor to content and pay to the said Complainer the soume of threttene schillings and four pennis money."

The reader will notice the delicate manner, in which what looks very like a breach of the 8th commandment, is spoken of in a legal document of that period. John the son of Alister " confessed " the intromission with the brown horse, but pled in defence, that he " took him away ordowrlie and nocht spulyed, but be vertue of the Act of Athell, boynd for ane better horse spuilzeat be the said persewar from the said Defender." Whether this was the truth, or whether though it were true, John the son of Alister was justified in seizing upon the Baron's broune horse, in lieu of the one taken by the Baron from him, or whether it was, that the Baron was the more powerful of the two,—the judge it will have been noticed, de-cerned against the said John M'Alister, not however ordaining him to return the horse, but to pay the Baron "thairfor," the sum of thirteen shillings.

The next notice we have of Shaws of Dell, is in the Valuation Roll of the Sheriffdom of Inverness, where in 1644, John Shaw (No. 6) is assessed at the sum of £66, 13s 4d, and in 1691, Alex-ander Shaw of Dell, (No. 7) at £66, 3s 4d.

Then we have Sir Robert Sibbald in his MS. (1680) preserved in the Advocates' Library—speaking of Rothiemurchus as " hold-ing of the Regality of Spynie, and as formerly belonging to the Schaws, who yet possess the parish, Alexander Shaw of Dell, (No. 7) being the head of the tribe. "The Schaws are able fighting men," he adds, " and acknowledge MACINTOSH to be their chieftain, and go under his banner." And lastly, we have James Shaw of Dell (No. 8) appearing along with 17 others, in the conference as to the Chieftainship between MACKINTOSH and CLUNY in 1726. His wife, we gather from the Genealogy of the Mackintoshes of Belnes-peck, was a daughter of Lachlan Mackintosh of Belnespeck.

The Historian of Moray was of the family of Dell, which family, there is strong reason for concluding, as is shown in a volume pri-vately printed, entitled " *The Dalrymples of Langlands*," (p. 88,) is now represented by John Shaw, Esq., Attorney in the High Court of Madras.* He is a member of the family of Shaws well known in

* Marion Shaw granddaughter of the Rev. Lachlan Shaw, Annalist of Moray, was married to Sir Alexander Cochrane, G.C.B., Admiral of the Blue, 6th son of the Earl of Dundonald. She and her niece (Mrs Jeffrey wife of Lord Jeffrey, and a

Scotland as having been for generations connected with Coylton and Ayr. They intermarried with the Dalrymples of Langlands; and hence the notice of them in that volume.

Their ancestor, the Rev. George Shaw, was Minister of Logie in Stirlingshire at the Revolution in 1688, but declined to change his creed and conform to Presbyterianism. He kept possession of his charge, for sometime after Presbyterianism was established. At page 86 of the volume last above quoted, we are told that " it appears from the Records of the Kirk Session, that they took proceedings to remove George, in December of that year; and there is an entry on 5th August, 1691, requiring him to return to them, " the utensils," meaning no doubt " the Communion Cups." Full details as to this family since their connection with the south of Scotland, are given in the said volume. One of them, the Rev. Dr David Shaw, was 60 years minister of Coylton—his father having been 52 years minister of Edenkillie in Morayshire. The former died in 1810, the latter in 1754. Dr Andrew Shaw, brother of Dr David of Coylton, was one of the Professors in St. Andrews when that city was visited by Dr Johnson. Boswell records that Johnson said of the Professor—"I took much to Shaw," (p. 95). He had a son, Andrew, who was minister of Craigie in Ayrshire, and was one of the Shaws alluded to by Burns in the " Twa Herds."

Dr Shaw of Coylton's eldest son, Charles, was clerk to the Justices of the Peace for Ayr. He died in 1827. One of his sons is Patrick Shaw, Esq., who was for a long period Sheriff of Chancery in Scotland. One of his daughters, Barbara, was the wife of the late Professor George Joseph Bell, Edinburgh; and the other, Marion, was married to Sir Charles Bell, Professor of Surgery in the University of Edinburgh. Miss Bell, daughter of Professor George Joseph Bell, has in her possession a valuable collection of MSS. and contemporary printed documents relating to the Rising of 1745.

great-granddaughter of the Historian) used to be spoken of as "cousins," by the Shaws of Ayr, with whom they enterchanged frequent visits, *(p. 88, Dalrymples-of Langlands)*.

Shaws of Delnavert, Guisclich, &c.

The information I have obtained as to the Shaws of Delnavert is
chiefly derived from the Macpherson MS. The first whom I find
noticed, is Alexander Shaw of Delnavert, who is put down in the
Genealogy of the Macphersons of Bealid, as having married a
daughter of William, 4th in descent from John, son of Ewan, their
predecessor. He lived, probably, in the middle of the 16th century. The Macpherson MS. gives few dates; but I have been enabled
to supply them in a good many instances, from finding the names
of the persons mentioned in the genealogies, occurring in authentic
documents and records of the period. For instance, in the Mackintosh MS. an Extract is given from the Register of the Provin-
cial Synod of Moray, of date 12th January, 1648, containing a
" Roll of those of Badenoch who were engaged in the Rebellion
under MONTROSE."

Shaws and Macphersons under the Ban of the Kirk for having Fought under Montrose.

In this interesting document there are four different classes, and
the punishment inflicted on each class by the Synod, varies according to the position in life, and the degree of "malignity" charac-
terising the unfortunate victims. Colonel Evan Macpherson of
Cluny, stands first in the Roll of persons summoned before the
Synod. He, along with Donald Macpherson of Phoyness, and
others, " were ordained to put on sackcloth, which they did,
acknowledging their hearty sorrow upon their knees, willingly sub-
scribed the Confession, emitted by the General Assembly at Aber-
deen, and solemnly promised in time coming to amend their former
miscarriages." In the second class, occur the names of William
Macpherson of Pitchern; William Macpherson in Pitmean; James
Shaw in Dunachten, and others. " In respect they were not leaders,"
they were ordained to make their repentance in "their own habit."
A third class, comprising Donald Macpherson of Nuid, Malcolm of Phoyness, and others, "in respect of their being less malicious," were ordained simply " to make their repentance in their own
Parish Kirk." In the most malicious class, which was simply re-

ferred to the Presbytery to "process and censure," as being "absent without excuse," I find "William Shaw of Delnavert, John Macpherson in Crathiemore," and ten others.

In another class, we find Andrew Macpherson of Cluny, father of foresaid Evan ; Angus of Invershie ; John of Nuid and others ; excused from compearing at the Synod, "on account of their age and inability to travel."

In addition to this performance of public penance before the Synod, several were ordained "in respect of having been present at bloody fights and joined with the bloody enemies," to appear in their respective Parish Kirks, Auldearn, Kingussie, &c. Amongst these were Col. Evan Macpherson of Cluny, Donald Macpherson, fiar of Phoyness, and James Shaw in Dunnachten.

The names of most of these will be found occurring in the following notes of intermarriages between Shaws and Macphersons.

Well has a modern writer spoken of the punishment undergone by those wild Highlanders as "a mock penance." Their confessions could not have been very hearty, and I fancy the indignity of appearing in sackcloth shirt, and on bended knee, had not very much affected them.*

I am rather of opinion, also, that the Ministers themselves had not been disposed to be very severe, on their "pugnacious and rebellious" Highland cousins. Very different was the punishment inflicted on those engaged in the rising in 1745.

Resuming the subject of early notices of Shaws of Delnavert and others ; in the MS. Genealogy of the MACPHERSONS OF INVERSHIE, I find that William Macpherson of Inveressie, (6th in descent) married a Shaw of Delnavert.

* In connection with the above penances, undergone by Highland Chiefs, I quote the following from Burton. "At this time," he says, "we hear of statesmen sitting for lengthened periods on the stool of repentance, and parish ministers re-enacting the part of Hildebrand with the Emperor. The Lord Chancellor, Loudon, made his repentance in the East Church of Edinburgh, with abundance of tears. . . . The earl of Dumferline gave satisfaction . . . sitting in his own seat in Dumferline, but not in sackcloth, on the stool of repentance at Edinburgh, as did the Earl of Crawford, Lyndsay, at the same time. History, vol. vii., p. 246.

She is the heroine of the Legend at p. 178 of Sir Thomas Dick Lander's "Highland Rambles." It occupies 54 pages of that volume. I shall give an abridgment of the story.

Legend of Macpherson of Invereshie and his Wife—a Shaw of Delnavert.

Macpherson of Invereshie was a "tall handsome Highlander, elegant in his manners, kind in his intercourse with all around him, but bold and determined in any difficult or desperate juncture." At the house of a neighbouring chief, he first met the lady, one of the chief's nieces, who was destined to be his wife. She had been educated in Edinburgh, had mixed "in splendid scenes at Court," and was a young lady of surprising "beauty and grace of mien." The moment her eyes met Macpherson's, a glamour came over him. He had previously resisted, it is said, the blandishments of many a Highland maid, and the efforts of many a Highland mother to secure him as a son-in-law. But this was a case of love at first sight. The lady had not only been of a gay, but also of a romantic disposition ; her latter characteristic prompting her to take moonlight walks at very late hours.

Whilst Invereshie was riding home one night, he was startled by her appearance, sitting on a grey moss-covered tomb-stone, among the ruins of an ancient chapel. There he wooed her and won her. But no sooner had they parted than dark thoughts crossed his soul. He dreaded that it was a sprite and not a human being with whom he had been conversing so lovingly. But with the morning dawn, however, reason resumed her judgment-seat, and reflection made him ashamed at his own weakness, in giving heed to the wild phantom thoughts which had crossed his brain, at the mid-night hour.

He easily gained her uncle's consent to their union, and the marriage-day came on. Just as the goblet had been drained to the health of the happy pair, the lady swooned away ; a great commotion ensued in the castle, and she lay so long inanimate (for hours it is said) that it was thought she was dead. Happily, how-

D

ever, she recovered her consciousness, and Invereshie took her to his home rejoicing.

Her habits of gaiety acquired in the South, did not accord well with the customs of the home even of a wealthy Highland Laird of that period. Troops of guests flocked to Invereshie. She went innocently on, in obedience to that bent which her education had given her, fancying only that she was doing her duty. Her tocher had been ample, but it melted rapidly away ; and the natural result of keeping open house, and giving expensive entertainments, ensued—Invereshie got into difficulties. Still the fascination exercised over him by his beautiful wife, was too powerful to allow him to interfere, or to remonstrate with her.

One day he chanced to meet his old nurse—one of those crones, supposed in old times, to be gifted with the second sight. The bent of his mind, as the reader may have gathered, was gloomy and superstitious, so she easily persuaded him that he was under the influence of a spell,—that it was not a human being to whom he had been married, but an evil spirit, who had taken possession of the body of his bride on their wedding-day. Invereshie dwelt on the thought, and it "*possessed*" him. In plain English, he had gone mad. One moonlight night he proposed to his wife that they should have a walk in Glenfeshie. No proposal could have been more agreeable to the lady. She at once consented, little dreaming of the dire thoughts which were agitating the brain of her husband. Arrived at a point, where their walk touched the verge of a precipice, overhanging the dark rapid waters of the Feshie,— in a moment he grasped her in his arms and threw her down into the stream. She did not sink, but floated on the surface, calling out— " Help, help, my love, my lord, it was accident ; save me, help me." " She floats," muttered Invereshie ; " by Saint Mary, then the old woman was right. Ha ! she struggles at yonder tree." He sprang from the rock to the margin of the stream, and scrambled towards the spot, whither the eddy had whirled the now sinking lady. She had caught, with a death grasp, by one frail twig of an elder sapling ; and, " Help, oh help," was now all she could faintly utter. " Help," said Invereshie, " Saint Michael be mine aid, thou canst well help thyself by thy foul enchantments, *thou hast already taken much from me, thou mayst e'en take that twig with thee too,"* and drawing from his belt his *skian-dhu,* he sternly divided the sapling at its very root. As it parted its hold, the lady disappeared among the rough surges of the rapid stream. And then, all at once, the veil with which superstition and madness had darkened the mind of her husband, fell from his eyes. " Holy angels, *she sank,"* he exclaimed with a maddening yell that overwhelmed the roar of the flood. "My love, my wife, I have murdered thee."

Resolute in purpose and daring in deed, he now dashed, in his right mind, into the foaming waters. Happily, he succeeded in rescuing the lady, and bringing her in safety to the brink of the stream. We may imagine the rest. A perfect reconcilment ensued, as well as a retrenchment of expenditure, and in due time she became the mother of Angus, ancestor of Sir George Macpherson Grant of Ballindalloch and Invereshie. Such is an abridgment of the Legend, as given by Sir Thomas Dick Lauder.

He is mistaken, however, as to the Christian name of her husband. It was not John, but William. He is, also, mistaken in saying, that John Macpherson was the Laird, who got the Charter of the lands of Invereshie. It was not John, but Angus, son of the marriage between William and Shaw of Delnavert's daughter, (*Macpherson MS. and Douglas' Baronage,* p. 360). This Angus got a Charter of the lands in 1643. He married a daughter of Farquharson of Brouchdearg, and had a sister, Margaret, married to Shaw of Reinachan in Rothiemurchus. He had also a brother, John Oig, whose son, the Rev. Thomas Macpherson, married Bathia Maxwell, daughter of the Bishop of Ross. Bishop Maxwell was consecrated in 1632.*

* Bishop Maxwell was afterwards made Archbishop of Tuam. On the 14th of Feb., 1646, he was found lifeless on his knees. He had been very active some years previously, in the compilation of the Scottish Liturgy, had maintained it against Presbyterian criticism, and said it for years in his own Cathedral of Chanonry. He was driven out of Scotland by the ban of the Assembly, and all but slain by the Romanists, when he first entered on his Irish See.—(*Scot. Eccl. Journal,* vol. ii., p. 77.)

Intermarriages of Shaws with Macphersons.

The above-mentioned Angus had a son, Thomas, the founder of the Macphersons of Killihuntly. They had a son, Donald, who married Euphie Shaw, daughter of Robert Shaw of Tordarroch, *(temp. Charles II.)* His (Angus') eldest son, William of Invereshie, fought under Montrose and was killed at Auldern.* His son, Sir Æneas, is the author of the various MSS. relating to the Macphersons, Shaws, and Farquharsons, from which much of the information now given in these Memorials is derived. The father of the above-named Robert Shaw of Tordarroch, was Æneas, who, along with many others, signed the Bond of Manrent to MACKINTOSH in 1609.

Another ancient branch of the MACPHERSONS was the family of PITCHERN, tracing from Donald, son of Thomas of Pitmean, *(temp. James V.)* His great-granddaughter, Mary, married Donald Shaw of Delnavert, who is mentioned by Sir Æneas Macpherson, as being one of the old men, alive when he himself was young, from whom he got his information in *" Vanitie Exposed."* The date of Donald must therefore have been *circa* 1600.

The brother-in-law of Donald, Alexander Macpherson of Pitchern, married Mary, daughter of Evan Macpherson of Cluny, and their grandson, William Macpherson of Pitchern (1648), married Margaret, daughter of said Donald Shaw of Delnavert. William Macpherson of Pitchern, was one of those censured by the Synod of Moray, in 1648.

I shall now give the intermarriages between the Shaws and the Macphersons of PHOYNESS and ETTERISH. Gillicallum Macpherson was the progenitor of the former, and " Thomas Roy " of the latter family. They were sons of Donald Macpherson, married to Jean Macpherson, daughter of Macpherson of Crubenmore. Thomas Roy was out in the Rising under Montrose (1647), and

---

* His name does not, of course, occur in the Roll of those cited to compear before the Synod at Forres. His father, Angus, was one of those excused on account of his age.

was censured by the Synod on that account. He is also mentioned by Sir Æneas Macpherson as one of his authorities in " *Vanitie Exposed.*" He married Isobell Shaw, daughter of Alexander Shaw of Guisclich in Rothiemurchus. It was the daughter of a subsequent Shaw of Guisclich, John Shaw, who was the mother of the famous Colonel John Roy Stewart of 1745 celebrity. Thomas Roy's son, John, married Janet, daughter of Evan Macpherson of Cluny, who was such a staunch supporter of Montrose. They had a daughter, Jean, married to John Shaw of Delnavert—probably the son of Donald. Jean's brother, Alexander, is given as one of the subscribers of a " Vindication by Macpherson of Badenoch to Duke of Gordon," in 1699, *(Spalding Club Misc.*, vol. iv. p. 166).

To return to the MACPHERSONS of PHOYNESS. Gillicallum (or Malcolm), and his son Donald, both fought under Montrose. The father, it will be remembered, was mildly dealt with by the Synod, " in respect he had been less guilty than the others." Donald's grandson, Angus of Phoyness, married a daughter of Shaw of Delnavert, probably John Shaw last above mentioned. Malcolm Macpherson is mentioned by Sir Æneas, as one of the old men whom he had consulted in the preparation of " *Vanitie Exposed.*"

With the MACPHERSONS of NUID, our intermarriages were not so numerous. About 1690, Donald Shaw, son of Robert Shaw of Tordarrroch, married Jean, daughter of Donald Macpherson of Nuid. She had previously been married to Mackintosh of Benchar. A grandson of Donald of Nuid, Lachlan, married in 1704, Jean, daughter of Cameron of Lochiel.

With the MACPHERSONS of ESSICH, there were two intermarriages : Donald Macpherson of Essich (*circa* 1610), married Effie Shaw, daughter of Bane Shaw of Tordarroch. Effie was sister of the Æneas Shaw of Tordarroch, who signed the Bond of Manrent to Mackintosh in 1609. Malcolm Roy, a younger brother of Donald of Essich, married a daughter of Donald Shaw of Delnavert.

The connection of the Shaws with the MACPHERSONS of DEL-
RADDY was more recent. There were two successive families of
Macphersons of Delraddy. The genealogy of the original family
is given in the Macpherson MS. It states, that Angus Macpherson
of Delraddy feued his lands of Delraddy, to John 2nd son of Angus
Macpherson of Inveressie and brother of William, who was killed
at Auldearn. John's grandson, Lewis Macpherson, was wadsetter
of Delraddie in 1745. He married Una, sister of Ewan Macpherson
of Clunie, of 1745 celebrity. His sister, Madeline Macpherson,
married Thomas Shaw of Kinrara, brother of John Shaw of Kinrara, who, with 14 others, was killed in cold blood on the field of
Culloden, the day after the battle. I have derived the information
contained in the above paragraph, partly from Douglas' Baronage
pp. 358, 361, Chambers' Rebellion, p. 432, and papers in a Chancery suit, arising out of a Deed of Settlement, left by Major
Robert Shaw, son of said Thomas Shaw of Kinrara.

Shaws of Kinrara.

In said process in Chancery, Thomas Shaw of Kinrara, is de-
scribed as "residing at the house of his relative Thomas Shaw of
Delnavert," so that the Kinrara branch must have been an offshoot
from the Delnavert branch. A Marriage Contract between William Shaw of Forneth and Isobel Shaw of Kinrara, dated at Kinrara, 25 August, 1751, bears to be written by William Shaw, son
of Angus Shaw of Delnavert, who also signs as a witness. There
is a tombstone to the last Shaw of Delnavert in the churchyard at
Rothiemurchus, dated in 1810. Miss Shaw of Shawfield is descended, through her grandmother, the foresaid Isobel Shaw, from
the Shaws of Kinrara.

The following account of the slaughter of Shaw, younger of
Kinrara, at Culloden, is taken from Bishop Forbes' Papers :—

. . . "The most shocking part of this woful story is still to come—
the horrid barbarities committed in cold blood after the battle was over.
The soldiers went up and down, knocking on the head such as had any
life in them; and, except in a very few instances, refusing all manner of

relief to the wounded—many of whom, if properly taken care of, would doubtless have recovered. A little house, into which the wounded had been carried, was set on fire about their ears, amongst whom was Colonel Orelli, a brave old Irish gentleman in the Spanish Service. One Mr Shaw, Yr. of Kinrara, had likewise been carried into another hut, with other wounded men, and had among the rest a servant of his own, who being only wounded in the arm, could have got off, but chose rather to stay, in order to attend his master. The Presbyterian minister at Petty, Mr Lauchlan Shaw, being a cousin of this Kinrara's, had obtained leave of the Duke of Cumberland to carry off his friend, in return for the good services the said Mr L. had done the Government. As he came near, he saw an Officers' Command, with the Officer at their head, fire a platoon at fourteen of the wounded Highlanders, whom they had taken all out of that house, and bring them all down at once ; and when he came up, he found that his cousin and his servant were two of that unfortunate number. I questioned Mr Shaw himself about the story, who plainly acknowledged the fact, and was indeed the person who informed me of the precise number ; and when I asked him if he knew, if there were many more murdered that day in the same way—he said, he believed there were in all twenty-two."—*Bishop Forbes' MSS. Edited by Mr Robert Chambers in Jacobite Memoirs.*

The original of the following Protection of General Wade to John Shaw of Kinrara, is in the Charter Chest of the MACKINTOSH :

" George Wade, Esq., Lieutenant-General and Commander-in-Chief of H.M. forces, castles, forts and barracks, in North Britain. By virtue of the power and authority to me given by His Majesty, I do permit and authorise you, John Shaw of Kinrara, in the county of Inverness, to keep, wear, and carry with you, upon any your lawful occasions, from the date hereof, to the 20th September, 1740, ye following weapons, viz., a gun, sword, and pistol ; your behaving all that time as a faithful subject of His Majesty, and carrying yourself peaceably and quietly towards the people of the country.—Given at Inverness, the 26th day of August, 1728. (Signed) GEORGE WADE. Recommended by the Lord Advocate and Col. Farquhar."

Errors in Douglas' Baronage.

Notices and Genealogies, more or less perfect, of most of the above named branches of the Macphersons will be found in Douglas' Baronage, pp. 360, 366. I find the Baronage very incorrect, when checked with contemporary documents in the Spalding Club Volumes. On the other hand, I find that the Macpherson MS. tallies with such documents in every instance. I shall give but one instance, and that a glaring one. *Ex uno disce omnes.*

In Cluny's Genealogy, in Douglas' Baronage, we have—

XIV.—Andrew Macpherson of Cluny (no date), succeeded by—

XIV.—John his brother, who gets a Charter of the lands of Tullich, &c., 1594, died in 1600, succeeded by his son—

XV.—John Macpherson who gets a Charter (1613) *de Tullich* &c., and is succeeded by his son—

XVI.—Ewan of Clunie who gets a Charter of Tullich, &c., in 1623, and dies about 1640 ; is succeeded by his son—

XVII.—Donald who gets a Charter of the lands of Middlemoir, in 1643, and was a staunch friend of Charles I.

Now it was Ewan, not Donald of Cluny, who was the staunch supporter of Charles I., and who did such splendid service under Montrose. " He was the first Scotsman," says the Macpherson MS., " who joined Alexander Macdonald alias Colkitto, when he came with the King's party out of Ireland." We find him fighting under Montrose in 1647, censured by the Synod of Moray, and made to kneel in sackcloth before them in 1648, *eight years after the Douglas Baronage puts him down as a dead man.*

Again, the Douglas Baronage gives us John, as father of Ewan. Whereas we find an Andrew Macpherson of Cluny, excused by the Synod from compearing before them, on account of his age, in 1648. In the Macpherson MS., we have Andrew put down as Ewan's father, thus agreeing with authentic Records of the period.

True, there is an Andrew, occurring in the Genealogy of the Douglas Baronage. But the Baronage makes this Andrew *die* previous to 1594. Where, let me ask (according to the Baronage) are we to look for the Andrew Macpherson of Cluny, who, we find in a public Record of the period, was alive in 1648 ?

It is well known that the family of *Nuid* merged in that of *Cluny*, and I fancy the Charters of both families have been applied to, for the steps in Cluny's descent, and names inserted in Cluny's Genealogy which belong of right to that of Nuid. I could follow this idea out, and I think, *prove it*, but this is not the place.

Chapter Third.

I HAVE now exhausted the sources of information, which have come into my possession since the previous portions of the Memorials were printed. For the sake of those, who have applied to me for copies of those portions, but to whom I was unable to supply them, I shall recapulate some of the particulars as to those Branches of the Shaws, of which the former portions of the Memorials treat.

The Irish Branch of the Shaws.

Having heard from Mr Shaw, Corgarff, of the existence of a tradition in Speyside, that a member of the Clan had emigrated to Ireland about the period of the Revolution in 1688, whose descendants, he had heard, now occupied a high position in that country, I ventured to forward a copy of the Memorials to the late Sir Robert Shaw, Bart., Bushy Park, Dublin, along with a letter, enquiring as to the origin of his family. He sent me in reply, a copy of the Pedigree of his family, in which the fact, that it had originally been a branch of the Clan Chattan, was duly recorded. He entered into the subject with the greatest keenness. His last directions to his brother, before leaving Ireland for France in the middle of February 1869, were—to keep Sir Bernard Burke in remembrance of a request he (Sir Robert) had made, that Sir Bernard would endeavour to find out farther information as to the original connection of the family with Scotland.

The family of Sir Robert traces its origin from a member of the Clan, WILLIAM SHAW, who was an officer in General Ponsonby's Regiment in the army of William III. For distinguished

E

services in Ireland against the rebel troops, both General Ponsonby and Captain Shaw, obtained grants of forfeited lands in Kilkenny and Tipperary. When General Ponsonby was wounded at the Battle of the Boyne, Captain Shaw carried him off the field. Capt. Shaw's great-grandson, Robert Shaw, sat in the Irish Parliament for New Ross, and voted against the Union. He represented Dublin in the Imperial Parliament from 1804 to 1826, and was created a Baronet in 1821. His son, the late Sir Robert, was distinguished as a scholar at Trinity College, Dublin. The Irish newspapers in noticing his death (which happened on the 19th February, 1869) all spoke of him in the most eulogistic terms, as a "patriotic citizen of Dublin, an indefatigable friend to the poor, and a most amiable, and in every way an excellent man." The present writer can only say, that he had come to the same conclusion as to his character, from his letters, before he had heard it from others. Nothing could exceed the kindness and the hearty zeal with which he entered into the subject of the Memorials of his Clan; and as the leading Inverness-shire paper remarked in recording his death—"He had a warm side to the 'Tartan' and to his ancestral country."

His brother, Sir Frederick—present Baronet and Recorder of Dublin—has, I am glad to say, taken up the subject no less warmly. Sir Frederick was M.P. for the city, and afterwards for the University of Dublin. He was legal adviser to the late Conservative Government, and (as a fellow-Clansman, Sheriff Shaw, Lochmaddy —who was unaware until recently of his ancestral connection with Scotland—writes to me)—one of the most formidable opponents who ever entered the lists in debate, against the late Daniel O'Connell. Sir Frederick Shaw married Thomasine Emily, granddaughter of Robert, first Earl of Roden.

The above was written in an Appendix to Part I. of Memorials in 1869.

It will have been noticed, that the documents which have since come into my possession, all point to the tradition of a migration of Shaws of the Rothiemurchus stock to Ireland. The same tradition is preserved in the family of Shaws of Coylton and Ayr, springing from Shaws of Dell, (*Dalrymples of Langlands,* p. 88).

There can be no doubt, therefore, that the distinguished Irish family, now represented by Sir Frederick Shaw of Terenure, may be rightly and truly claimed by the Scottish Shaws as united to them in the bonds of a common Clanship.

I may add, that it is to Sir Frederick Shaw that the members of the Clan are mainly indebted for the printing of this Edition of the Memorials, and that he is as pleased to be reckoned one of our Clan, as we can be to claim him. (*See Burke's Peerage and Baronetage for Genealogy of the Family.*)

Shaws of Tordarroch.

The following account of the Tordarroch Shaws, was supplied to me by my dear friend and kinsman, Mr A. Mackintosh Shaw, a worthy member of the Tordarroch race :—

" This branch of the Shaws is deduced from ADAM, second son of James Shaw of Rothiemurchus, who was the son and successor of Shaw Mor Coriaclich. Adam obtained from the Chief of Mackintosh, his kinsman, a wadset of Tordarroch in Strathnairn, and his posterity were known as the Shaws of Tordarroch. The Tordarroch Shaws appear to have little or no connection with their cousins of Rothiemurchus—perhaps on account of their being situated at such a distance from them. But although they have not attained to such historical eminence, as these said cousins, they have always been a family of some estimation, and intimately concerned in most of the doings of the Mackintoshes, living as they did in the country of that clan. The family is still largely represented, both at home and in Canada, but they no longer hold the property, as the wadset was given up in 1810, by Alexander Shaw, the last of Tordarroch, to Sir Æneas Mackintosh of Mackintosh. The family also held the property of Wester Leys.

Æneas Shaw, father of the Alexander just mentioned, was engaged in the rising of 1715, and was an officer in the battalion of Brigadier Mackintosh of Borlum, as was also his brother. Being taken prisoner at Preston, he was first confined at Newgate, and then

sent to America. By the intercession of friends, he was set at
liberty, but was compelled to give bond in heavy securities for his
future allegiance and faith to the reigning family. He kept his
word during the '45, but on the eve of Culloden, his wife, fearing
he might yield to the temptation of going to fight for Charlie, took
the precaution of secreting various portions of his wearing apparel.
My great-grandfather (his son) then a boy, used to relate, in after
years, how restless his father appeared, and how he saw numbers
of men crossing the river and passing the house in disorder.
Æneas' daughter, wife of Farquhar Macgillivray of Dalcrombie,
also remembered soldiers being quartered in the house after the
battle, and their being present at the performance of Divine worship,
which was held in the house. When the country became quiet,
Æneas Shaw was made a Magistrate, and his three sons received
Commissions in the Army, the second, Æneas, rising to the rank of
Major-General."

" Genealogy of Shaws of Tordarroch.

JAMES SHAW, son of Coriaclich, had a son, ADAM, the progeni-
tor and founder of the Tordarroch branch. He was father of
ROBERT, who was father of BEAN, father of ANGUS (Ay or Æneas).
ÆNEAS signed the bond of Manrent given by the Chief of Mackintosh in 1609, by the heads of the various banches of the Clan
Chattan. After him came ROBERT, and then ALEXANDER, whose
son, Æneas above-named, was out in the '15 and taken prisoner at
Preston, along with his brother, Robert. They were both officers
in the regiment commanded by Brigadier Mackintosh of Borlum.
A "William Shaw" was quartermaster. In the list of officers,
there are twelve Mackintoshes, three Farquharsons, three Mac-
gillvrays, two MacBeans, and two Macqueens, (*Antiquarian Notes by
Fraser Mackintosh of Drummond*).

Æneas had five children—

I.—ALEXANDER, Lieutenant 60th Regiment (Royal Americans),
afterwards Lieutenant-Governor of the Isle of Man.

II.—ÆNEAS, Captain 6th Regiment, afterwards Major-General,
and a member of the Legislative Council of Canada.
Æneas served in the first American War, as Captain in the

Queen's Rangers (64th Regiment), was afterwards a Major-General in the army, and a member of the Legislative Council of Upper Canada. He died of fatigue in the war of 1813. He left a large family, mostly settled near Toronto, at Oakhill *i.e.* (in Gaelic) Tordarroch.

III.—JOHN, Major 68th Regiment, was killed in action with a privateer on his voyage to the West Indies.

IV.—ANNE.

V.—MARGARET, married Farquhar M'Gillivray of Dalcrombic.

The above-named Alexander had ten children:—(1) ÆNEAS, died a Major in the Army; (2) JOHN, a Major-General; (3) HENRY also an officer in the Army; (4) CHARLES, Lieutenant, 17th Regiment; (5) CLAUDIUS, Lieutenant, Royal Artillery, served in the Peninsular War, and afterwards on the Niagara frontier, was colonel in command of Artillery in the British Legion in Spain in 1835, and is a knight of the orders of San Fernando and S. John of Jersulem; (6) DUNCAN WILLIAM, Major, 20th Bombay N.I.; (7) ANNE; (8) ELIZABETH; (9) MILLICENT; (10) AUGUSTA."

Mr A. Mackintosh Shaw is the grandson of the above-named Claudius.

J. A. Shaw Mackenzie, Esq., of Newhall, Ross-shire, is the eldest son of the above-named John, and so the head of this branch. On succeeding to Newhall through his grandmother, he had to take the name of Mackenzie.

The Crathinard Shaws.

It is 160 years since Crathinard passed from the Shaws, and, indeed, it was only held by them for two generations; but I designate the branch, as to which I shall next give a few particulars, by that name, because of the prominent position held in our Clan history by my ancestor, DUNCAN of CRATHINARD.

As shown in a former portion of these Memorials, the Crathinard Shaws, and the Inchrory Shaws, both trace their descent from Alister Ruadh of Achnahaitnich, a brother of Allan the outlawed chief. Alister was noted for his determined resistance to the

Grants, who came in his brother's place as possessors—though certainly not *in his time*—as occupants of Rothiemurchus. Alister's son, JAMES SHAW of TULLOCHGRUE, was born probably about 1590. He was the last of that branch of the Shaws, of which the writer is a member, who lived in Rothiemurchus (*circa* the year 1600). A manuscript, found amongst the papers of George Shaw, merchant in Dantzic in 1760, and eldest son of William, seventh son of Duncan of Crathinard, states that "James Shaw, father of James Oig, set up at Tullochgrue," and that "he married a daughter of Farquharson of Invercauld."

The record in George Shaw's manuscript of this marriage is confirmed by the independent testimony of the Farquharson Genealogy. In that genealogy we find the following entry:—"Finlay Mor's son, ROBERT of Invercauld," (by his second wife, Beatrice Gardyne), "Married the Baron Reid in Strathardle's daughter, by whom he had four sons, Finlay, John, Alexander, and William, and two daughters, whereof the eldest married William Glas (Grey) Mackintosh in Badenoch, the other JAMES SHAW in Rothiemurchus."

The above is extracted from "The Genealogy of the FAQUHARSON, brought down to 1733, by Alexander Furquharson, Tutor of Brouchdearg," and known among Scottish genealogists as "THE BROUCHDEARG MANUSCRIPT."

I am inclined to believe that the "James Shaw of Dunachten" censured, as we have seen, for his share in the Wars of Montrose, was the same as James Shaw of Tullochgrue. The only families of importance in the district at the time were the Shaws of Daill, the Shaws of Delnavert, and the old dispossessed Shaws of Rothiemurchus. The Shaws of Delnavert were well represented in those wars, by William of Delnavert, who declined to submit to the dictation of the Presbyterian Synod of Moray. Alister of Auchnahaitnich, too old to go to the wars, is said to have had an eager desire to have an interview with Colkitto; which desire, tradition tells us, was gratified, when Montrose passed with his army through the wilds of Rothiemurchus.

It is not likely that the son of such a father would be deaf to the call upon his loyalty, made by the great Montrose; and I am therefore led to the conclusion that the James Shaw of Dunachten, censured by the Synod of Moray for the share he had in the wars of Montrose, was no other than the James Shaw, who, according to G. Shaw's MS., afterwards "*set up*" at Tullochgrue.

G. Shaw's MS. records the marriage of "James Oig," (*young* James) son of James of Tullochgrue, to "Miss Machardy, niece to the Earl of Marl, and heiress of Crathie." In the "*Book of Annualrentaris and Wadsttaris within the Schirrefdome of Aberdein,* 1633, we find "JOHNE MACKHARDIE IN CRATHINARD," (*Spalding Club Miscellany,* vol. iii. p. 139). James Oig is also designated in the MS. as "James Shaw of Crauhinard." On his removal to Deeside, the headship of the tribe had devolved on the head of the Shaws of Dell, in whose hands we found it held in 1688.

Here, I must not shrink from making known, what I believe to be the truth, that though the above quoted MS. states, that Miss Machardy was niece to the Earl of Mar, I have heard that she was in reality, only a *reputed* daughter of Machardy's, being an illegitimate daughter of the Earl of Mar. An old aunt of mine, gone to her rest since I first entered on the compilation of these Memorials, and who used to tell me long stories about the Shaws of Rothiemurchus when I was a child, gave me this information, when I questioned her on the subject.

The son of James of Crathinard was DUNCAN OF CRATHINARD. He was born in 1653, and died in 1726. He was the father of a numerous offspring, and a man of note in his day and generation. His mother's connection with the Mar family procured him, I suppose, his appointment as Chamberlain to John, 11th Earl of Mar. A Protection, in which he is so designated, was given to him by General Mackay, and is dated 26th June, 1690. It states that he had "hitherto behaved himself loyallie and dutifully to the present Government, and had hindered all his tenants, and servants, from joining those in rebellion against their Maties. King William and Queen Mary," and that therefore "these are prohibiting and discharging all officers and soldiers of their Maties. armys to trouble or molest the said Duncan Shaw, his family, tenants or servants, or to take away spoyll or meddle with any of his or their goods, gear, cornes, cattell, or others whatsoever, belonging to them. As they shall be answerable upon their peril. Given at the camp at Auchintoul on the head of Gairne, the 26th June, 1690. (Signed) H. MACKAY." The original of this document is now in my possession, having been given to me two years ago by my trusty friend and kinsman, William Shaw, Esq., Finegand. The Earl of Mar was then, and for a long time afterwards, attached to the reigning Government, and was in fact only fifteen years of age, having succeeded his father Charles the year before. Duncan seems to have changed sides with his master, their previous attachment having been, like that of may others, a matter of necessity rather than of choice. He also raised and commanded a company of twenty men, for protection against "the Catterans," one of the companies which were the precursors of "the Black Watch," which was not regularly embodied till 1739. His obtaining a protection from General Mackay of Scourie, seems scarcely reconcilable with the strong exhibition of Jacobite principles afterwards made by his family; but there can be no doubt that he was a Jacobite at heart. His ward, the Earl of Mar, being at the Revolution of 1688, a mere boy, Duncan acted the wiser part in "keeping his clan at home." That "a Protection" was more than needed in his district, after "Dundee's spur was cold," is terribly evidenced by what Mackay wrote to Lord Melville on 29th August 1690 :—"I burnt 12 miles of a very fertile Highland country (Strathdee), at least 1400 houses, but had no time to go the length of Braemar." But the "pious Mackay" was on the winning side, and so his persecutions of poor Highlanders are made to sink into insignificance, when compared with the sufferings of Covenanters, in the popular histories of the day.

Duncan's first wife was a daughter of Forbes of Skellater. His second wife was a daughter of Farquharson of Coldrach, by whom he had seven sons and five daughters.

I.—JAMES of DALDOWNIE, who married (1st) a daughter of Young of Birkhill; (2nd) a daughter of Farquharson of Waterfowl. His eldest son, Duncan of Cortachy, was factor to Lord Airlie. He was great-grandfather of Dr George James Shaw, Bombay Army; Major David Shaw, Adjutant - General, Pegu Division, Bengal army; and Doyle Shaw, R.N.

II.—JOHN of RIVERNEY, who married a daughter of Farquharson of Brouchdearg.

III.—DONALD, an Officer in the Dutch Army.

IV.—DUNCAN of the Balloch in Glenisla. He married first a daughter of Small of Dirnanean, and next a daughter of George Farquharson of Coldrach—a captain in the Rising in 1715, whose mother was Mey Farquharson, daughter of INVEREY. Duncan was great-grandfather of William Shaw, the writer's father; William Shaw, Finégand; James Shaw, Skaithmuir; Gordon and David Shaw, Merchants, India; Charles Shaw, Sheriff-Substitute, Uist;* John Shaw, at one time Speaker in the Legislative Assembly of New Zealand.

V.—ALISTER of the AUCHAVAN married first a daughter of Murray of Binzean, and second a daughter of D. Shaw of Delnavert.

VI.—FARQUHAR, great-grandfather of the Rev. John Shaw, Priest of the Roman Catholic Church at Rutherglen, married a daughter of John Shaw of Glenclunie in Braemar,

VII.—WILLIAM of BROUCHDEARG married first (in 1738) Agnes Bannerman, heiress of Fornetb in the Stormont; and second (in 1751) Isobel Shaw, daughter of J. Shaw of Kinrara. He was grandfather of Miss Shaw of Shawfield, and great-grandfather of David Shaw, W.S., and of Frederick Shaw, Dundee; and also of William Shaw, the writer's father, through Margaret Shaw, who married

* Sheriff Shaw has in his possession two relics of Prince Charles Edward—one is a very elegant knife-case, which was given as a keepsake to his maternal ancestor, Dr M'Leod, brother of "RAASAY." This relic is engraved and noticed as being in Mr Shaw's possession in "Chambers' Book of Days," i. p. 520. The other relic is a very valuable miniature portrait of the Prince, which came to Mr Shaw through the same channel.

F

her second-cousin Charles, grandson of Duncan No. IV. He suffered much from the privations he endured in hiding from the pursuit of the Hanoverian troopers.* The writer's great-grandfather used to carry his food to him, when he was in concealment in a cave in one of the hills of Glenshee.

Five of the above-named sons of Duncan of Crathinard, were "out with PRINCE CHARLIE;" the two who remained at home being James the eldest, and Duncan the fourth son. Alister was in Lord Airlie's Regiment. He was wounded at Falkirk, but slew the dragoon who wounded him, and fought afterwards at Culloden. At his funeral, Lord Airlie planted his foot on his faithful follower's grave, and said—" Here lies one who never turned his back on a friend or an enemy."

Duncan's claymore was long preserved in the family. It was taken, I believe, by the late Captain Shaw (formerly tenant of Linross, Forfarshire) to America. He had the bad taste to have it shortened by about a third, in order to bring it within the regulation length of the period.

Duncan of Crathinard's brother-in-law, by his second wife, was Captain Donald Farquharson of Coldrach, who fought under DUNDEE in 1688, and who was again " out," with his son George, in the Rising under the Earl of Mar in 1715. A " cousin " of Coldrach's was Peter Farquharson, Colonel of the Marrmen in 1715. Peter's brother, James Farquharson of Balmoral, led the clan in 1745, (*Brouchdearg MS.*)

How Duncan of Crathinard managed to keep his clan at home in 1688, with such relatives and connections, and afterwards to

* In connection with this matter, I may narrate an incident worth preserving on record. A troop of Hanoverian dragoons found their way as far as Dalrulzion, in search of the Laird, who was not far off. In order to give warning to him, as well as to the rest in the Blackwater, who had reason to apprehend danger, Miss Rattray entered into conversation with the drummer in the kitchen, and pretended not to know the use of the drum. The soldier having explained its use to her, she expressed a wish to hear the sound ; which desire the soldier politely gratified. The officer in command came in breathless haste to the back-court, to stop the procedure. But it was too late. The crags above Dalrulzion re-echoed the sound, and the country-side was warned.

extort a Protection from General Mackay, it is difficult to understand.

The name of only one of Crathinard's daughters has been preserved—Grizel. She was married to Donald Farquharson of Balnakillie, a grandson of Lachlan Farquharson of Brouchdearg.

Duncan sold Crathinard to Farquharson of Invercauld sometime before his death. He died at Crandard in Glenisla, formerly the residence of the M'Combies, and in old times a place of great strength. He was buried within the precincts of the ancient Church at Glenisla; but his grave in the burial-ground of the Shaws, is to the southwards of the present Church, which was not built on the exact site of the old.

Shaws of Inchrory.

The Shaws, formerly of Inchrory, of whom old William Shaw at Corgarff is now the worthy representative, trace from John Shaw, brother of Crathinard. John's son, Alister,* was I.st of Inchrory,

---

* Under the title, "A Story of 1746," in the Ettrick Shepherd's Tales, an account is given of the manner in which Colonel John Roy Stewart, Shaw of Inchrory, Loch-garry, and a Captain Finlayson, discomfited a party of dragoons sent in pursuit of them. I heard the story when I was a child, in the house of John Shaw of the Balloch in Glenisla, an old patriarch of the race, long since gone to his rest. John Roy Stewart was surprised in the house of Inchrory, whilst his friends were in concealment among the neighbouring hills. Holding up his bonnet at the corner of an aumry, which was visible from the window, the dragoons discharged their carbines at it, fancying that it was his head. John Roy then opened the door, slew the first two who attempted to enter, one after the other, with a sweep of his broadsword. Another was cut down a few yards from the door, when John Roy's companions having made their appearance, the other two took to flight, pursued by the Jacobite Colonel, kilted as he was, on the horse of one of the dead dragoons. John Roy Stewart had served in France, was a man of fine presence and great strength, and a most accomplished swordsman and musician. He also wrote some touching verses and songs. Those on the progress and results of the Rebellion have been elegantly translated from the Gaelic, in which they were composed. They appear in a recent work by Dr Rogers of Stirling, and breathe the most deeply rooted hatred towards the Duke of Cumberland.

He was tenth in descent from his ancestor, Walter Stuart, Baron of Kincardine, son of the Earl of Buchan, who was son of Robert II. of Scotland.

A cave in the face of a rocky eminence, called Craigowrie, in Kincardine, where he hid after "the '45," is still called "Uaimh Iain Rhuaidh," John Roy's Cave.

In one of his poetical compositions, he inveighs very strongly against the Campbells and red-coats who were in search of him.

as to whom many curious anecdotes may be found in Sir Thomas
Dick Lauder's Legendary Tales. Some of these are amusing
enough, but Sir Thomas has missed the true conception of Inchrory's character. I shall give one anecdote, in a version which
was told to me, by one who had never read the tales.

Alister was famous for his breed of stag-hounds, and the then
Lord Fife having become desirous of possessing a dog of that particular breed, made overtures to Inchrory, through his factor, for
the purchase of one. "Sell my dog," said Inchrory to the factor;
"does Lord Fife think I would sell my dog. Tell him I would as
soon sell my wife." In those days, it would have been considered
equally mercenary for a gentleman to sell his game. But times
are changed.

It was not long until a gillie made his appearance at Lord Fife's
Shooting Lodge, with Inchrory's compliments, and a dog for his
Lordship.

I find I have omitted to mention in their proper place at page
45 :—Charles Shaw, Finégand, great-grandson of Duncan (No.
IV.); Alexander Shaw, Bolyell, great-grandson of Farquhar (No.
VI.); and James Shaw, Auchenree, great-grandson of William
(No. VII.)

A great-grandson of James of Daldownie, (No. I.) was James
Shaw, long a partner of Messrs Caddell and Co., Booksellers, Edinburgh. He was one of the very few in the secret of the author-
ship of the Waverley Novels. His nephew, James Shaw, is a manu-
facturer in Dundee.

Chapter Fourth.

It now remains for me to notice a few matters connected with the Clan and its history: the Badge, the Arms, the Tartan, the Clan Rant, the ancient Castle of the Chief at Loch-an-Eilan, &c.

Badge.

According to Logan* and Colonel J. A. Robertson,† the SUAICHEANTAS or Badge is that of the Clan Chattan, the Red Whortle Berry; instead of which, however, boxwood is often worn, the leaves of the boxwood and red whortle berry being very much alike in appearance. It will have been seen, however, (p. 13) that an older authority than either Logan or Robertson, Sir Æneas Macpherson, states that the Badge of the Shaws was a "tuft of heath or heather." This is the badge always worn by my "cousin" "Finniegand," one of the few Shaws who still, now and then, "wear the garb of old Gaul."

Arms.

QUARTERLY First and Fourth, Or, a LION RAMPANT gules, armed and langued azure: Second and Third argent, a FIR-TREE growing from a mount in base proper; and on a Canton Argent, a DEXTER HAND couped fesswise, holding a Dagger Gules.

CREST: A Demi-Lion Gules, holding in the Dexter-Paw a sword proper. MOTTO: *Fide et Fortitudine.*

The Lion Rampant is common to all the branches of the Clan Chattan, claiming to be descended of MacDuff. The Fir-Tree is

---

* Logan, Clan Shaw.
† Robertson's Historical Proofs on the Highlanders, p. 413.

common to the Shaws and Farquharsons, "in commemoration," says Sir Æneas, "of Rothiemurchus from whence they came, and where grow so many firs." In a Survey of the Province of Moray (p. 263) published in 1798, it is stated that Rothiemurchus signifies the great plain of firs (*Rathad-mór-guibhais*). One of the old forms of spelling is *Rathamurchas;* and I am inclined to think that the derivation of the word is from *Rath*, a round earthen fort or stronghold; the fort having been the old Stychan* or "Doune" of Rothiemurchus; and the meaning would be the fort among the great or tall pines. "*Rath*" is found variously combined all over Scotland, as in Ratnamurlich (*Rath-na-mor-loch*) the *Rath* or fort near the large loch ; Rathmorail, the majestic fort. Hence, also, Balmoral (for *Balmorail*) the majestic town.

Tartan.

The MacDuffs and Shaws have always worn the same Tartan. It is of course better known as the MacDuff, than as the Shaw Tartan.

Rant of the Clan.

The old Rant of the Clan—Rothiemurchus Rant—was the tune for which Burns wrote the song, "Lassie wi' the Lint-white Locks." Rant is an old Scotch word for a "lilt" or melody.

> How heartsome is't to see the rising plants,
> To hear the birds chirm o'er their pleasing *rants.*
> —*Gentle Shepherd.*

In "Lassie wi' the Lint-white Locks" the third part of the tune is omitted.

Spelling and Pronunciation of Chattan and Quhele.

Burton tells us, in a Note to his History (iv. p. 137) that in old Scotch *Quh* was used to express the sound of *wh.* The *Ch* in Chattan and Chewill, is pronounced in Gaelic, like *ch* in *loch* (as a Scotchman pronounces it). Accordingly the old chroniclers and lawyers, as we have seen, rendered these names by the words Quhattane and Quhele, the nearest approach they could make to the Gaelic sound of *ch.* The letter *y* was used of old for *th.* The

---

* Preface to Spald. Club Misc. iv. p. xxvi.

(Clan) *Yha* of Wyntoun would, therefore, be the equivalent of *tha* or *thai*, and perhaps be his way of spelling the Gaelic (Clan) Dhai.

The Name Shaw.

As Logan justly remarks, the Gaelic name, *Saidh*, *Sheach*, or *Scheauch* has nothing to do with the Saxon *Shaw*, signifying a "small wood." The Saxon *Shaw* had been adopted as the sound most nearly resembling that of the Gaelic word : just as *Æneas* has been adopted for *Angus*, *Charles* for *Tearlach*, &c.

The word in Gaelic seems obsolete ; but those who know the language have told me that it means "sprightly, proud, or spirited." Perhaps the fairies of the Highlanders, the *Daoine Shith* or *Shi'*, (men of peace) may have something to do with it.

Having done so far with facts, I now proceed to treat of certain matters of more or less interest, in which a degree of Romance will be found mingled with the realities of my theme. And first as to

Farquhar Shaw of the Black Watch.

The following poem by my friend Mr Colin Sievwright, Author of a volume entitled "Sough of the Shuttle," appeared in the *Montrose Standard* some months ago. It was preceded by the following introductory paragraph :—

"The following verses," he says, "are intended to illustrate a very touching episode in the history of the Black Watch. That brave regiment had been spirited to London, under pretence of being reviewed by the King. But their real destination, in utter contravention of the terms of enlistment, was the colonies or other foreign service. This having oozed out, the proud spirit of the Gael could not bear deceit, and so the regiment, under the command of Farquhar Shaw and the brothers Macpherson, set off for the land of the heather. They were overtaken at Northampton by a force of cavalry and infantry overwhelmingly superior, and, after holding out in an entrenchment for three days, they had to succumb. They were taken back to London, when the three ringleaders were tried and executed. See *Chambers' Book of Days* and *Grant's Legends of the Black Watch*, for farther particulars : "

Air—An ancient Gaelic melody.

The wind o'er the mountains is wailing in sadness,
No longer the valleys are smiling in gladness,
For Scotland is fallen, her banner is drooping,
The sons of the Gael to the stranger are stooping ;
    The foot of the Saxon
      Has trod on the heather,
    And the glory departeth
      For ever and ever.

Our chieftains are slain, and our Princes are banished.
The power and the pride of the clansmen are vanished ;
And Cumberland's butchers return from their slaughters
All drunk with the blood of our sons and our daughters ;
    Wherewith they have blackened
      The bloom of the heather,
    Oh ! the glory departeth
      For ever and ever.

Ah ! Scotland my country, thy noblest defenders
Are lured from thy hills to the land of the strangers,
Condemned, like the convict, to cross the wide ocean,
And die among slaves, for their loyal devotion ;
    Thy malison follows
      The heartless deceiver,
    But the glory departeth
      For ever and ever.

But hark ! they remonstrate, the soul of each hero
Revolts at the baseness of England's vile Nero,
The SHAW and the Brothers MACPHERSON together
Are leading them back to the land of the heather ;
    They love the old country,
      Each mountain and river,
    But the glory departeth
      For ever and ever.

Arraigned in court-martial, how noble their bearing,
They ask, but in vain, a dispassionate hearing ;
In vain they protest that a loyal obedience
In the red field of battle will prove their allegiance ;
    Their doom is from life
      And its trials to sever,
    Oh ! the glory departeth
      For ever and ever.

Once more the dread silence the president breaketh,
And nobly in answer brave Farquhar Shaw speaketh ;
" Man, what is your faith ?" " 'Tis the faith of my fathers,
Long, long ere a Saxon foot trod on our borders ;
    But now on the heather
      Your minions may gather,
    And the glory departeth
      For ever and ever."

" You have lived ?" " As please GOD and the blessed St. Mary,
I hope to depart to the kingdom of glory,
A Catholic faithful—my head never drooping—
No man ever fearing—to none ever stooping !
    Alas ! for my country
      Where blooms the red heather,
    For the glory departeth
      For ever and ever."

" To none say you ?" " No one save JESUS my SAVIOUR,
Who pleads at the FATHER's right hand for his favour,
To guide the poor wanderer through every temptation,
And bring him in peace to the land of salvation.
    But oh ! Loch-an-Elian !
      Oh, Isle of my fathers !
    All your glory departeth
      For ever and ever.

" Now, doomed from the earth and its glories to sever,
I look for a glory that lasteth for ever,
A bright blessed country, where no true believer
Will crouch at the footstool of Saxon deceiver ;
    The home of the true heart,
      Beyond the dark river,
    Where the glory endureth
      For ever and ever."

Since the former portions of these Memorials were written, I have learned some farther particulars concerning Farquhar Shaw. A Mr John Shaw, who returned to his native country after more than half-a-century's absence in America, and who spent a few months in Grantown last summer, wrote to me (in reply to a letter of enquiry which I had addressed to him, along with a copy of the

G

Memorials) :—"As to Farquhar Shaw, who was shot in the Tower in May 1743, he was born and reared at the end of the Bridge of Alvie, and was my father's uncle. His mother was a daughter of Keppoch's, who was married to my great-grandfather." Mr Shaw also writes to me, that his own father was regarded as head or Chief of the Shaws in Rothiemurchus, in the end of the last century. He was probably, therefore, one of the Shaws of Delnavert, but as his letter was not written to me until after his return to America, and as he omitted to give me his address, I am precluded from making farther inquiries.

Commenting on what I had said* in the Memorials, as to the attachment of the Shaws of former times, to the Church of such of the White-Rose Scots, as were not Roman Catholics—the Church commonly called Episcopal in Scotland, Mr Shaw writes:— "I am surprised to hear that the Shaws were so devoted Episcopalians. I always understood that they were staunch Catholics. When you were at Rothiemurchus, you might have seen the Iron Cross lying in one of the little enclosures in the corner of the Churchyard, that some bigot had taken from my forefathers' heads, and had tried in vain to break."

Between my American clansman and myself, there certainly is no difference on this point. The Shaws of old had doubtless been as staunch Roman Catholics as they were afterwards Episcopalians; which latter appellation, however, some of their descendants do not recognise as the true and proper designation of the members of the Church to which they belong, as a branch of the Church of CHRIST.

---

* I had written—"There was a small chapel at Persie, some 3 miles from the southern base of Mount Blair, until the end of last century, to which all Crathinard's family for a long time resorted. The top of the altar used in it is in the possession of my father; and the chalice, with the name and arms of Rattray of Dalrulzion engraved upon it, is now in use at the Episcopal Church at Meigle. The paten is in the possession of Dean Torry, Coupar-Angus. It is told of my great-grandfather, James of the Lair, that he declined to shake hands with the clergyman on coming out of Church on the Sunday when King George was first prayed for. Miss Shaw, of Shawfield, has in her possession an old Prayer-Book which was used by her mother in the Chapel when she was Miss Rattray of Dalrulzion. The chalice is very old, and had been given by the Rattrays to the Church.

No doubt, it is its distinctive designation in this country. But in ceasing to be Roman Catholics, our forefathers did not believe that on that account they were one whit the less Catholics. Every time we say the Creed, we profess our belief in the HOLY CATHOLIC CHURCH.

The preceding pages contain accounts of all the leading branches of the Clan, so far as known to me. I doubt not there are many Shaws scattered throughout the world, who may be able to show their connection with one or other of them. Only the other day, I learned that one of the Tordarroch Shaws, Captain Donald Shaw of the 86th Regiment, had come to the knowledge of the previous edition of these Memorials, through a friendly notice in the *Inverness Courier*. On coming home, he made endeavours to procure a copy. During the progress of this edition through the press, I notice the death of Brigadier-General Sir Charles Shaw, Knt., Knight-Commander also of the Portuguese Order of the Tower and Sword. He was a brother of Patrick Shaw, Esq., formerly Sheriff of Chancery.

I may here mention, that Sir Benjamin Brodie, whose paternal ancestor came from Banffshire, tells us in his Autobiography, that his grandmother was a daughter of Dr Peter Shaw, who had followed the fortunes of the Stuarts, and accompanied King James II. abroad. Sir Benjamin speaks of his ancestors on both sides as "staunch Jacobites," (*Autobiography*, p. 1).

There can be no doubt that Dr Peter Shaw, and a cousin of his, also a physician, of whom Sir Benjamin speaks, had been members of the Clan.

I have in my possession a correspondence in 1760, between a Dr William Shaw, London, and G. Shaw, Dantzic (of the Crathinard family). The doctor was evidently a relative of the merchant, but I cannot trace the connection. A Gideon Shaw of the Customs, Edinburgh, and a Captain Daniel Shaw, of whom I know nothing, also crop up in the correspondence.

Burial Place of Coriaclich.

I found, on the occasion of my visit to Rothiemurchus last summer, that our American kinsman had placed a new stone slab over Coriaclich's grave, with an inscription commemorating his exploits on the Inch at Perth. In that inscription, Coriaclich* is called "Farquhar Shaw;" and Mr Shaw informs me he was always so designated in the district in his (Mr Shaw's) young days. Be that as it may, I am not sure but that I should have preferred that the rough old grey slab, with its four corner-stones, and the tradition in the country as to whose grave they covered, coupled with the other tradition as to the dire punishment, which, it is said, is sure to be inflicted by the hand of the guardian spirit of the Shaws—the Bodach-an-Dune,—on any one who may be bold enough to remove them,—I am not sure but that I should have preferred that these old memorials should have been left without any modern addition, to tell to future generations the story of the prowess of Coriaclich.

The burying-ground of the Shaws has ever remained separate and distinct in the Churchyard of Rothiemurchus. They have still a heritage in Speyside, but it is the heritage of a tomb. The grave of Coriaclich is in the centre of a group of the graves of his kindred. None but Shaws have ever been buried there, and there are few remaining in the district now, to be buried, when they die, beside the dust of Coriaclich. No written title exists, on which the race could found, to prove their claim to the proprietorship of this burial-place ; but there it remains at the eastern end of the Church of S. Tuchaldus, an impressive witness to the reality of their bygone history.

It is said that in days gone by, when an old patriarch of the Grant family, who had enclosed a sepulchre for himself at the corner of the churchyard farthest removed from the Shaws burying-ground,—was asked the reason for building it in such a remote corner,—his reply was, that—" He was an old man, and that at the resurrection, he would like to get the start of the Shaws. They had never agreed in life, and he was sure they would not agree then."

* Coriaclich means " Bucktoothed."

The Bodach-an-Dune.

The *Bodach-an-Dune*, or Ghost of the Dune, is the name of the guardian spirit, who, tradition tells us, presides over the fates and fortunes of the Shaws. His ministrations to them are said to be always friendly. He is mentioned under the head "Superstitions" in the Annals of Moray, (p. 344.) When the Shaws were dispossessed by the Grants, it is said that the voice of the Bodach was heard making great lamentation on the Dune. His song, in Gaelic, ran thus—

> Ho! Ro! theidd sin sa chiomachas,
> Theidd sinn o fhonn 's odhige;
> 'Sged thug iad uainn ar duchas,
> Bidh ar duil ri cathair na firinn.

which is, literally rendered—

> Ho! Ro! we go into captivity;
> We go from lands and strongholds;
> But though they have taken our country from us,
> We shall hope for the City of Righteousness.

or more freely—

> Ho! Ro! as exiles we go,
> From our lands and strongholds, away, away.
> But we trust, though out-thrust
> By an earthly foe,
> To reach the City that lasts for aye—
> The City of Peace, for aye, for aye.

Another spirit, who was said of yore to haunt the wilds of Rothiemurchus, was the dread Lamh-Dearg, the awful spectre with the bloody hand.

It is of this spectre that Sir Walter Scott thus writes in Marmion—

> For such a phantom, it is said,
> With Highland broadsword, targe, and plaid,
>   And fingers red with gore,
> Is seen in ROTHIEMURCHUS glade,
> Or where the solemn pine-trees shade
> Dark Tomantoul and Auchnaslaid,
>   Drumouchty, and Glenmore.
>
>   —*Marmion*, Canto iv. 22.

As the ghost, it is said, insists upon engaging in single combat with every one to whom he vouchsafes an appearance, he must be a peculiarly unpleasant spirit to encounter.

Akin to this, is the superstition mentioned by Mrs Ogilvy in her Highland Minstrelsy, (p. 99). She tells us of a haunted tarn under the shadow of Schihallion.

> Where, dancing on the sullen loch,
>   A ghostly troop there went,
> Whose airy figures floated high,
>   On the thin element ;
> And fiercely at each others breasts,
>   Their mock claymores they bent.

Chapter the Last.

In the former edition of the Memorials, I gave an account of two successive visits which I made to Loch-an-Eilan. Such accounts are, of course, of too personal a nature to possess any other than a very limited interest. But, nevertheless, they afford me an opportunity of describing the scenery of the ancient home of our forefathers to my fellow-clansmen. The circumstances attending my last visit were of so picturesque a nature, as to be deemed worthy of being thrown into verse by my friend, Mr Colin Sievwright, to whom I narrated them. The verses will be found well worthy of insertion in the Memorials of the Clan.

The visit was made in company with my wife, who has since gone to her rest, and my two eldest sons. The sun was shining brightly when we reached Aviemore, by the Highland Railway, a little after mid-day. But we had scarcely left the station, when we heard the sound of distant thunder. As it gradually rolled nearer and louder in the surrounding glens, we thought it best to remain at Aviemore until the storm should pass away. It continued to rumble—now faint, now loud—until the afternoon, when it became more distant. We then started for Loch-an-Eilan, which is about two miles distant from Aviemore. It continued to roll at intervals, as we wended our way through the woods, until we came within sight of the gorge or glen between Ord-Bane and Cairngorm, in which the Loch is situated. This gorge is about a mile long, by three quarters of a mile broad, and is encircled on all sides by hills, except one, these hills being spurs of Cairngorm, the blue summits of which tower aloft at six miles distance. As we entered the narrow pass, through which it is approached, with Ord-Bane rising almost precipitously on our right, and the hill of Tulloch-grue on our left, it was shrouded under a murky thundercloud, which completely cut off from our view the summits of the adjoining heights, and we therefore seemed to be entering a huge mountain prison. Nevertheless, we pressed onwards towards the Loch, hoping that the worst of the storm was over. And our hopes were so far realised. We enjoyed the scene in spite of the gloom, and amused ourselves by awakening the sounds of the ancient echo, formed by the castle walls. If the sound be loud enough, it is sent back by the castle walls to the neighbouring rocks and hills, so that in a still day, it is six or seven times repeated. At last, I shouted out the old motto of our race, " *Fide et Fortitudine ;*" and I confess I felt somewhat startled, if not awed, when—with the last notes of my voice—a grand thunder-peal, apparently directly overhead, joined its awful reverberations. My wife and I looked at each other in silence, endeavouring to realize to the full, the glory and the grandeur of the scene. And we all sat more silently on the banks at the edge of the Loch for sometime, apprehensive that we were to have both thunder and rain. There had been only a very few drops of rain at intervals during the day. This, however, was the last peal which we heard except one, which rumbled forth faintly, about a quarter of an hour afterwards, and died away like " the sound of a lost battle," in the far, far distance, over by Glenmore.

My sons and I then rowed to the Castle ; and on our return to the shore, the scene was changed as if by a magician's wand. Rain had been falling heavily as we were rowing towards the shore, but we had scarcely landed, when the sun broke through the cloud, and a magnificent rainbow spanned the surface of Loch-an-Eilan, the Castle appearing as if framed in a glorious semicircle, under the centre of the bow. Never shall I forget the beauty and the glory of the scene. Words utterly fail one in the attempt to describe it. To use the language of another,* in expressing the difficulty of finding words to describe a beautiful landscape :—

* The late John Shaw Soutar, Esq., Dunfermline, a relative and very dear friend of the Author.

" Who has not felt in gazing on such a scene, how utterly futile must be the attempt to *describe* it to others—how miserably feeble and inadequate the power of language to convey to other minds, any just conception of the numberless elements of beauty, combined to make up the sum of loveliness, that ravishes the senses ; or to impart to them a share of those emotions and impressions, profound yet pleasing, by which your own mind is so mysteriously affected. A catalogue of material beauties indeed, the tongue or pen *can* supply, but there are other elements, too fine and subtle to be conveyed by secondary and artificial *media*. Where is the glorious light shed down by the sun upon the scene ? the rich profusion of colour on wood, and rock, and water,—the vocal melody that " comes o'er the ear " from the unseen recesses of the mountains and the woods,—the peaceful and intense stillness which pervades the whole scene, falling with such gentle power on the human spirit itself, elevating and purifying its aspirations, and saying, with calm authority, to the stormy passions within its mysterious depths—" Peace, be still." No, these are things over which the pen has no power."

Just as the rainbow spanned the lake, the thought struck me, of the curious coincidence between the picturesque circumstances attending our visit, and the fact, that my sons were, I believe, the first of the ninth generation, from our forefather, Allan, who had visited Loch-an-Eilan. Till the ninth generation from Allan, the race, it will be remembered—according to an old prophecy, handed down in its traditions—were to be exiles and under a cloud ; and then there was to be brightness. I could not help recalling this old prophecy, at the sudden outburst of sunshine on the scene, coupled, as it was, with the appearance of the rainbow, ever regarded as the most significant emblem of peace, since the day when " it first spoke peace to man." The cloud was over us, but, lo ! there was " the bow in the cloud." Some allege that now and then there is an apparent exhibition of a sympathy between the material and the spiritual worlds. They believe that—

> There are more things in heaven and earth than we
> Can dream of, or than nature understands ;
> We learn not through our poor philosophy
> What hidden chords are touched by unseen hands.

The poet at all events, has assumed this sympathy in the following verses :—

H

Loch-an-Eilan, sad and lone,
Long has thy day of pride been gone ;
Rothiemurchus knows no more
The race that dwelt upon thy shore ;
Scattered now in every clime,
Waiting the appointed time,
When they shall return to thee—
Fide et fortitudine.

But, Loch-an-Eilan, to thy shore,
See the Shaws draw nigh once more ;
And darkly dense o'er Cairngorm,
Rolls an awful thunderstorm ;
And deadly still, as in a shroud,
Sleep thy waters 'neath the cloud,
As they launch the boat on thee—
Fide et fortitudine.

They would see—for they have come
From far to see their fathers' home,
Come to see its crumbling walls,
To stand within its silent halls ;
Offspring of the ancient race,
They love their fathers' dwelling-place,
Hoary ruin though it be—
Fide et fortitudine.

Heedless of the lowering gloom,
Fearless though the thunders boom,
See, they stand upon the shore,
Where so strong in days of yore,
Loch-an-Eilan's castle stood,
Begirt by Loch-an-Eilan's flood,
When the Shaws dwelt mid the free—
Fide et fortitudine.

The eagles,* and the eagles' nest,
Are gone from Loch-an-Eilan's breast.
The dark green pine is seen no more
On fated Loch-an-Eilan's shore ;

* Until within the last two years, there was an eyry on one of the towers of the
castle, in which eagles had hatched their young from year to year, for at least
fifty years previously. They were scared by the wood-cutters. As the pines are
now all cut, and the wood-cutters gone, its pristine silence now reigns at Loch-
an-Eilan.

But still the Echo lingers there;
They raise its wild notes in the air,
And one cries—" *Echo, answer me!*
Fide et fortitudine."

And, lo! from out the vault of heaven,
In thunder, is an answer given:
The castle walls send back the cry,
The thunder blends in grand reply;
With clamour loud the crags resound,
Now here, now there, now all around;
The ancient Echo answers free—
Fide et fortitudine.

And now the ninth of Allan's race
Has stood in Allan's dwelling-place,
And, lo! the thunder-cloud is riven,
Lo! the glorious bow of heaven,
Painted by the HAND DIVINE,
Spans the home of Allan's line;
From the curse the race is free—
Fide et fortitudine.

O'er the living and the dead,
Nine times thirty years have fled,
On the viewless wings of Time,
Since the day when Allan's crime
Brought upon the ancient clan,
Retribution's direful ban,
And the weird of sin to dree—
Fide et fortitudine.

The sun shines forth—the storm breaks;
The cloud, the mountain side forsakes,
A rainbrow bright is seen to rest
On Loch-an-Eilan's glittering breast,
Say, speaks it not in tones of peace?
Yes, from the curse there is release,
Once more the ancient race is free—
Fide et fortitudine.

FAITH AND FORTITUDE prevail:
Bodach, cease thy mournful wail,
Cease to sing thy doleful lay
On the cairn old and grey;

With a joy inspiring strain,
Bid the Shaws " arise again,"
Let their watchword ever be—
*Fide et fortitudine.**

I have, of course, inserted the preceding verses more on account
of their beauty than of any belief I should be so presumptuous
as to entertain, that there was any such connection between our
visit and the exhibitions in nature, by which it was accompanied,
as the Bard of the Clan has *imagined.* The coincidence, however,
was so striking, that one cannot help giving the imagination a
little rein; and on such coincidences, the heart and the memory
both love to dwell.

Here I bring these Memorials to a close. It will easily be seen
that what I have written, is only a condensation of the materials in
my possession. To any one desirous of obtaining additional information, I shall be very glad to supply it.

---

* Some of my fellow-clansmen always speak of me now as the " Sennachie "
(Seanachaidh) of the Clan. Mr Sievwright has certainly earned the office of our
Bard.

In Memoriam.

AND now it only remains for me, to end this little work, with the following Inscription, to the memory of one mentioned a few pages previously, united to myself by the nearest and dearest tie in life, who has been unexpectedly removed, during its progress, from the shadowy to the cloudless clime. But for the thought of closing it thus, I do not think that I could have had the heart— for a long time—to write the chapters, which remained to be written, when she was taken away. Apparently in perfect health, she saw the first chapter finished the night before she died. Loving her own country with all an Englishwoman's love ; glorying,* as was natural, in her English descent ; able, as she was, to point out in her lineage, an ancestor who fought at Agincourt, another who was knighted by King Henry VIII. at the battle of the Spurs, and another who raised a troop of horse for Charles I,†—she was nevertheless intensely Highland in her feelings and sympathies, entering thoroughly into the sentiment of the poet, that—

> Nowhere beats the heart so kindly,
> As beneath the tartan plaid.

She was brought up as a child amongst the hills of Athole and Strathearn, and she dearly loved the people, amongst whom her early years were spent. In this as in all other matters, her heart kept perfect "time and tune" with mine.

As Sennachie of the race, I venture to give myself the sad satisfaction, of thus preserving in its Records, her memory and her name.‡

* "The glory of children are their fathers." Proverbs xvii. 6.

† Parochial Topography of Wantage, Berkshire ; *in loc.*, "Clarke of Ardington," and "Wiseman of Spersholt, pp. 53, 144, *(Parkers, Oxford, 1824.)*

‡ If it should seem strange to some, that in these paragraphs, I should depart from the reserve, which they would themselves be disposed to keep, in speaking of those who are gone, I can only say, that I follow the bent of my nature and of my race. Sir Walter Scott beautifully describes and explains this peculiarity of the Celtic temperament, in his account of the funeral of the Chief of the Clan Quhele, in "The Fair Maid of Perth." This leaf is, of course, only affixed to copies of the Memorials intended to fall under the eyes of my relatives and friends.

THESE MEMORIALS OF THE CLAN SHAW,

I LOVINGLY INSCRIBE TO THE BLESSED MEMORY OF MY WIFE,

Maria Elizabeth Molyneux Shaw,

WITH THE EARNEST PRAYER,

THAT I WHO WROTE THEM, AND ALL WHO MAY READ THEM,

MAY ENTER AT LAST, WITH HER,

THROUGH THE GOLDEN GATES, INTO THE ETERNAL CITY,

INTO THE PRESENCE OF HIM WHO SITS ON THE THRONE,

ROUND WHICH THERE IS A RAINBOW LIKE UNTO AN EMERALD,

AND OVER WHICH,

THERE IS A SKY WHICH IS NEVER CLOUDED—

THE HOME OF THE TRUE HEART,

BEYOND THE DARK RIVER,

WHERE THE GLORY ENDURETH,

FOR EVER AND EVER.